WILD TIME

'*Wild Time* is a genuinely intoxicating night in the woods. Generous and witty, sexy and extremely smart, it torments Shakespeare with such lascivious glee and trips nimbly through the theatrical canon, leaving stardust & honeydew in its wake. To see the universe expanded out in prose, but also subverted and punked and stripped down and re-focussed, is a constant joy. I've never read anything like it.'

STEWART PRINGLE
Dramaturg, National Theatre

'I was laughing literally out loud. The pages that authors Biggin and Cooper hammer out are quite – astounding. I still can't get it out of my mind.'

ROBERT RAYMOND

'Funny, entertaining and ambitious, showing *Dream* in a whole new light, *Wild Time* approaches its source material with a sly, postmodern, punk aesthetic. In this way, it acts as a feminist and sex-positive critique of the original, and playfully engages with the ideas and methods of theatre in inventive and unexpected ways. Much of the novel's success is down to Biggin and Cooper's command of and love of the English language. The novel deftly switches through a number of tones and registers, from lyrically poetic to salacious to wryly humorous. Their kinetic dialogue is witty, fast paced and memorable. Bristling with new ideas and an anarchic style that is very much its own, with its bawdy humour, sharp dialogue, and imaginatively staged set pieces, it's easy to imagine the Bard himself enjoying this take on his work very much.'

THE FANTASY HIVE

'Wildly enjoyable, lavishly queer and written
with such humanity and tenderness. I adored it.'
CHRIS GOODE
Writer & Theatremaker

'Funny and mischievous, *Wild Time* is
a delightful reinvention… a treat for lovers of
theatre and the fantastical'
E.J. SWIFT

'A lusty reimagining of *A Midsummer Night's Dream*,
Wild Time spins you at arm's length in the middle of its heated
embrace. Transgression is at its heart: this new version does
its best to rip off the shackles of its originator, but pays
homage to it too by breaking as many rules as it can – just as
Puck and his cohorts are want to do. It's like being in a really
fun, messy party where I want to be friends – and maybe
more – with them all… erotic and direct, joyful and funny,
Wild Time entices as much as it shocks. There are dangerous
pleasures to be had here, if you're bold enough.'
HONOUR BAYES
Writer & Critic

'a witty homage to Shakespeare's *Dream*…
raunchy, irreverent, transformative'
CAROL CHILLINGTON RUTTER
Professor of Shakespeare & Performance Studies, Warwick

'I loved this book so much.
A world of consensual desire, intergalactic tactility,
theatre ancient and contemporary. Wow.'
ANDY KESSON
Early Modern Scholar, Roehampton

'Separately and together, Rose Biggin and Keir Cooper
have transformed pole-dancing, *Don Quixote* and the
short-lived Second Spanish Republic into scintillating
punk theatre. With *Wild Time* they move in the opposite
direction, weaving a lusty, rumbustious novel from
Shakespeare's *Dream*. You might think this play had
undergone all possible mutations in the past century, but no:
Biggin and Cooper breathe new magic into this supposedly
"universal" story. Out goes Shakespeare's misogynist
revenge-porn and in come polyamorous revels, a throng
of wanton Amazons, and a queen of the forest bower
whose erotic encounters spread joy across the firmament
and pleasure across the page.'
MADDY COSTA
Writer & Critic

'This book promises an alternative *A Midsummer Night's
Dream* "as never seen before" and it definitely delivers.
If you are looking for an experimental text that packs
a lot of punches, this may be just what you need.'
BRITISH FANTASY SOCIETY

Also by Rose Biggin

Books
Immersive Theatre and Audience Experience (2017)

Theatre & Performance
BADASS GRAMMAR:
A Pole / Guitar Composition in Exploded View (2016)
Plunge (2015)
The Very Thought (2014)
Victor Frankenstein (2014)

Also by Keir Cooper

Books
A Handbook for Creative Practice (2012)

Theatre & Performance
Republica (2017)
BADASS GRAMMAR:
A Pole / Guitar Composition in Exploded View (2016)
Don Quijote (2013)

WILD TIME

by Rose Biggin & Keir Cooper

Surface Press

Paperback Edition

Surface Press

First published in summertime 2020
Surface Press. London

Surface Press is run by a community of artists in London and publishes
books, video and music. Starting in 2019, this is the fourth item under the press
and the debut novel. For further details or to get in touch contact directly
at surfacepress@gmail.com

A CIP record for this book is available from the British Library

ISBN 978-1-8381182-1-1 Hardback
ISBN 978-1-8381182-0-4 Paperback
ISBN 978-1-8381182-3-5 eBook

Text set in Fournier

This book has been supported
by kleine steinfelder galerie

Printed and bound by Lightning Source
Cover Design & Text Setting: Rose Biggin & Keir Cooper

To mischief

Contents

Openings

When the wind comes over the city from the ocean, it brings crystals of salt that settle on cheeks and eyelashes. If you're in the right place at the right time, either on the moonlit sand or some rising ground, beside the temple or the peach trees, you can gaze into the firmament and watch infinity unfold in a silent eruption. A great fresco decorating the sky.

All manner of phenomena up there; forever in flux, spontaneous, total. The turbulent heavens dressed up as single grains of sugar to our naked eye.

Which brings us to think about proportion: as with electrons shattering entire star systems; snapping worlds apart. Illimitable though they be but little. Galaxies succumb and collapse in on themselves while the lure of the moon pulls the edges of entire oceans this way and that.

The universe is a blanket, under which dreams are had and adventures are instigated, dark and warm and stained with stars and time. And as a blanket, it fits to our shape.

Everything moves. The arms of a spiral galaxy open up like a wildflower responding to the sun. The sequence of the stars is transient. A dozen points of light forming the constellation of a colossal figure, suddenly overlaps with a burst of supernova colour, and acquires a billowing pair of donkey ears.

We're in an ancient world, now; where gods and heroes are resident. And creatures called fairies saunter from one reality to another. In the blink of an eye we join the story.

Beginners on stage please —

The Aegean Sea was stroked over with liquid gold as the sun drew low to the horizon, preparing to escape and leave the city to it for the night. Locusts droned over the roof tiles, gliding by a marble statue where a great black kite stood preparing for the night-hunt with ready appetite. There was a steady creak in the orchards, open to the cool wind that rolled down from Mount Olympus. The whole city was waiting with bated breath, too excited to sleep, because tomorrow was going to be a big one.

Then there was a moment of bright white, a lightning flash, backlighting the trees of a forest on the Mediterranean. And the place was suddenly alive with movement and voices.

Sex Gods

'That was a bit much!'

'Yeah — not gonna be invited back soon are we?'

'Well there was quite a few of us.'

'It really picked up didn't it?'

'Will we have time to go to the beach, do you think?'

'Let's ask in a minute.'

'Did you see the marbles by the port? So tasteful.'

'We'll take one back with us when we go.'

The party arrived into a clearing that was dominated by an ancient fig tree. Titania looked over its huge twisted trunk, where a velvety moss had spread through the ridges in the bark. She nodded with satisfaction.

'Okay then,' she said. 'Let's make this place our own.'

The team sprang into action: laying out materials on the floor, carrying large items between them, discussing how best to interpret the space.

Buttermilk was securing sections of the thicket with direction from Fuchsia, who was straddled over a high branch.

'What do you think?' she called from above.

Titania gave her the thumbs up. The fairies were making progress. She helped Lullaby hang lanterns about the first tier of branches, jointly agreeing on aesthetic decisions.

'Nice work everybody — you're doing a beautiful job.'

Beside her was a peach tree, its low-hanging branches already overloaded with fruit. Two fairies passed by, heaving a considerably-sized log through the area, and positioned it artistically in the terrain.

She twisted a peach on the bough until it came off with a gentle click and made the branch sway, then took the hand of the beautiful young man by her side. She called out to the others.

'I'm going to hang out with the Changeling under the massive tree.'

'That's fine,' shouted Blossom, who was in its top branch, supervising. Although the fairies weren't finished up there, Blossom cupped her hands around her mouth and announced: 'That's break everyone!'

Titania looked at the Changeling, who was waiting calmly, hands on his hips and looking very casual. There was a confidence to his shoulders, and his body was as smooth as if it had been newly polished. He wore a piece of cotton, delicately printed, that bared his hips, and at some point one of the fairies had picked a red flower and placed it lovingly in his hair. 'My word,' she said, leading him beneath the tree. 'You're *completely* gorgeous, you do know that?'

He brushed off the comment with a bashful smile. It was a very well-practiced streak of coy. She tucked a loose lock of hair behind his ear.

The Changeling raised a hand and gently laced his fingers with hers. 'It's lovely to take a moment with you,' he said. 'Tell me again about tomorrow.'

Titania let go of his hand and playfully slapped him on the shoulder. 'You know it all!'

'I still like hearing it,' he said. He reached out towards her hand again and she fluttered it away.

'Say please, then.'

'Please,' he said.

Titania couldn't help herself. 'Very well,' she said, and the figs grew riper on the tree.

'Don't distract me then.'

The Changeling waited attentively.

'Tomorrow we're off to a wedding,' she said. 'The husband-to-be is the great Theseus. Ruler of Athens. Renowned the world over for feats of tremendous strength and bravery, now dedicated to statesmanship; busy with charity work. Fantastic bone structure.'

'He sounds like quite the guy,' said the Changeling. 'And who's making him feel lucky?'

He moved slightly as her hands stroked his body, her fingers playing over the cotton.

'Hippolyta,' she said. 'Queen of the Amazons.'

'The Amazons!'

'They're amazing. Impeccable warrior tribe, stuntswomen, strategists. Listen to this: they fire arrows backwards — while on horseback!'

'What talent,' he said.

She trailed her fingers over his chest. 'Riding at full gallop...

'Landing the target...

'... At any distance.'

The Changeling stretched out as he breathed in. 'Are the arrows on fire?'

'Sometimes they are.' Titania tapped him on his chest. 'Any more questions you must ask Hippolyta yourself. She'll be eager to meet you, of course.'

The air changed in the clearing. A subtle shift, Titania felt it. 'And I'll tell you who else is.'

There was a movement in every leaf like a shudder, a golden dart far above as a comet sailed over — and between the tall white trunks of two poplar trees stood the King of the Fairies.

He leaned nonchalantly against one of the trunks.

'My Queen,' said Oberon. 'And how was India?'

Titania let go of the Changeling's hand, and she and Oberon came quickly together with springing steps.

Oberon held her lightly at the waist and looked at her with love. A small pair of horns sat just over his ears, protruding through his hair. 'I heard you caused quite a stir out there.'

'Of course we weren't about to go entirely unnoticed,' she said. She placed her arms around his neck. 'This guy knows some really interesting people. You'd have loved it!'

Oberon raised his eyebrows. 'You'll have to tell me every detail.'

He brushed her cheek with his lips, and as her heart expanded with the pleasure of it a brand new iridescent beetle was invented in the highest branches of the poplars. It opened its wings and zipped away into the sky.

She opened her eyes.

'How rude of me! You haven't been introduced.' She held her arm out and gestured with her fingers. '*This* is the Changeling,' she said.

The King of the Fairies began an elaborate formal bow, by which time the Changeling had stretched out his arm for a handshake. They both attempted a correction, and ended up mirroring the problem.

'Let's just hug,' said Oberon, pulling the Changeling in for a squeeze. Then he held him out by the shoulders, as if appraising a fine work of art.

'More handsome than your message had me hope,' he said, addressing Titania without taking his eyes from his new friend. His gaze flickered across the Changeling's chest, down to the cotton, back to his face. 'You seem like one of those people who goes running a lot.'

The Changeling nodded. 'Every morning. Mixed terrain, three hills minimum.'

'He's extremely disciplined,' said Titania.

Oberon signalled to the Changeling and given the go-ahead, stroked endearingly with his fingers, caressing over the Changeling's ribs — the Changeling laughed a little at the tickling feeling.

'Well it's clearly working for you,' said Oberon. 'Ooh! You could go along the beach perhaps.'

'In your swimming things,' added Titania.

A nearby fern rattled about, sprigs and branches knocking together. A voice from inside said, 'Take me as well!'

Oberon broke off from the Changeling and turned to Titania. 'There he is!'

From the clump of spiky dry leaves emerged a new figure, bounding into the clearing. He stood there, beaming at everyone.

'My dear Puck,' said Oberon. 'Where've you been?'

'There's a lot going on in this forest!' said Puck. 'Remind me to tell you about the thing I saw.' He waved brightly at Titania, who blew him a kiss.

Puck's hair was sticking out at all angles just like the fern.

'But now here I am!' he said. He skipped closer. 'Is this the

7

new Changeling then?' Titania nodded. Puck cocked his head for an examination, narrowing his eyes.

'Can I have a lick?' he said.

'Go on,' offered the Changeling.

Puck grinned and turned back to face Titania and Oberon. 'I like him!' He stuck his tongue out at the Changeling and waggled it around.

Oberon glowed as he stared at the Changeling with adoration. 'We can spend all the time we need learning from each other.'

Titania frowned, just a little.

Oberon laughed happily and his voice took on a silken, lovestruck edge. 'It's going to be such an adventure to have you living with us,' he said. He caught Titania's eye. 'What's wrong?'

She was standing very still. 'He isn't living with us,' she said.

'Come again?'

She looked at Oberon's confused face. 'He's not living with us.'

Oberon blinked. 'You said the Changeling was our present?'

'Yes.'

'But now I'm ready to unwrap him and you're looking at me funny.'

'His *appointment* is our present.'

'Exactly!'

'So then — he's only with us tonight.'

'I don't understand.'

Titania saw the problem. 'He's not a gift for us,' she explained patiently. 'I said his appointment would make the perfect gift *from* us.'

She stared at him.

'His being at the palace,' said Titania. 'That's our gift to them.'

Everyone took a moment, broken only by Puck's footsteps as he padded to the Changeling and took his hand.

Oberon finally twigged. 'What? Our wedding gift? But that's silly!' he said, complaining. 'Place the Changeling in a different court?'

'He'll be perfect with Theseus and Hippolyta.'

'So I'm only here to look him over and say "hello and bye again"? He's such a rare find! We can't send him away?!'

'We'll spend tonight with him,' said Titania helpfully. 'One night between us — all the sweeter — then he goes off and fills the Athenian court with our blessings.'

Oberon turned to the Changeling with a pained expression.

'Yes, what she said — here tonight, then the palace,' nodded the Changeling with factual assurance.

Oberon looked as if he had just received a message from the tides that they were no longer prepared to go in and out.

'I thought you knew the plan,' said Titania. 'I thought we were both excited.'

'I'm excited!'

'Not now Puck,' said Oberon.

Titania folded her arms and cocked her head to one side. 'So you want to cancel at the very last minute and think of a totally new gift idea?'

'I mean, yes maybe! I don't know!' Oberon ran a desperate hand through his hair. 'Surely we can give them something else,' he said. 'Bedsheets?'

'We're not giving them bedsheets.'

'Special fairie ones?'

Titania rubbed her forehead. 'Let's rewind. Obviously, I'm not about to let a gifted Changeling pass us by entirely.'

'Sure.'

'Tonight we all enjoy each other's company.'

'Right.'

'And tomorrow he is appointed to his new position.'

Oberon waved his hands about emphatically at no one in particular.

'I know we get a lot of love from Changelings, and them from us,' said Titania. 'This time we express that love by placing him with dear friends who'll benefit from his appointment.' She put her hands on her hips. 'Oberon, I went all the way to India to sort this out. I've arranged it all.'

'He's one of a kind,' said Oberon, his voice dull with defeat. 'Look at the slope of his shoulders, the muscles of his back. Look at that definition there.'

Puck performed a neat leap onto the Changeling's back. The Changeling hutched him upwards and held gently onto his feet.

The Changeling spoke up again. 'I've been gladly awaiting these fairie revels. It's a huge debut for me. Tomorrow everything begins anew anyway.' Puck's hands were resting gently on his head.

Oberon closed his eyes as if gravely wounded. 'Listen to how charming and diplomatic he's being.' He shook his head. 'I can't bear this!'

'His gifts are too precious to keep to ourselves,' said Titania. She reached a hand towards him. 'We needn't argue. Let's have tonight.'

But his face had become drooping and sad. Oberon took a

few steps back until he stood alone and isolated in the middle of the clearing.

'If I'm being entirely honest with you here,' he said, 'I'm not really feeling in the mood now.'

They paused, at an impasse.

Oberon folded his arms. Titania looked at him astonished.

'That's ridiculous,' she said.

'No it's not. I'm responding appropriately to a ridiculous situation.' Oberon continued irritably. 'We've been waiting for this — he'd be entirely suited to join with us — and now you've arranged for him to be elsewhere there's nothing to be done. Titania, I'm dealing with severe disappointment. So I'll take my leave if you don't mind!'

And he turned and set off the way he had come. Puck leapt from the Changeling's back, landed lightly on the ground and scampered after Oberon, and soon their shapes were lost among the shadows of the forest.

Titania stood staring after them.

The Changeling gave an embarrassed cough and ran his thumb down the edge of his wrap of cotton. 'Seems like someone's got a case of the *deary-me*'s.'

'Fuck's sake,' said Titania.

*

Let's leave these ones here a moment
and turn our eye to the heavens...

The Laws of Pornodynamics

The smallest grains of space float suspended, sprinkled over everything; lavish, loose. And these little crumbs of spacetime, popping into awareness, turn up pinkened and keen, pushing gently at the universe's edge. Although these newcomers are far smaller than every tiny part of atomic things, they spill in handsome numbers and always the edge pushes back; the winds roll and the overall shape answers as its grains are swept.

This galaxy here is freewheeling across the universe like a rogue firework. It lurches and fishtails as it covers distance. The splay of redshift spreads further out and tinges the margins. We spot a cosmic mirrorball of a billion stars: corkscrewing over time on a stem of inexhaustible fabric, twisted and forever tautened. At its perfect centre is a dense pool of nothing leading to an unimaginable colossal black hole. The galaxy's glittering arms fan out from its middle, pulling the stars around it, super-massive as it turns.

In a quadrant near north-0.03 a planet glows brightly against her galactic coat, the heavy blackness of space wrapped around her like mink. She throws an occasional glance at the pulsars that glint in the night, she winks at them and they return her acknowledgements.

She transmits in bleeps and deep wavelengths. She is huge, a gas giant: rings swoop gracefully over her midsection, and she sits firm in the curving frame of spacetime, bending it under her. A small number of satellites have picked up the faintest of her traces, and logged her as Hel3na.

The fabric of everything has an aesthetic appeal that rewards Hel3na's attention; she takes a pleasure in its overlapping, rippling geometries. The ultrafast movement of this galaxy barely registers at her frequency, even as it careens madly across the universe like a loose tyre. Her surfaces remain untroubled; her pressures heavy, constant.

Pulling at her focus is a faint tremor. It stirs the smudging patterns through her soft pastel rings. A binary star is behaving strangely, dipping in and out of view. Hel3na enjoys the sight for a moment: eventually she breaks silence.

—   Oh Hello. Nearly didn't clock you there. Are you staring?

A conversation is on the cards now and it's almost as if who says what is mutable. The new star-set decelerates: acts of fission making sparks in front of him.

—   Well that all depends.

—   Does it?

—   On if you'd have me decent or true.

—   Can't I have both?

14

Hel3na ripples at this, her surfaces bounce. She's surprised to hear him speak so candidly.

She moves through the galaxy at ever greater speed, dipping and surging, keeping her eye on the binary star. She bristles and her patterns change on her outsides, gasses whirling like marbled paper.

She continues the exchange...

—   You're not shy are you? I love making new friends.

—   Friends?

—   Let's not get ahead of ourselves.

Hel3na gets the impression that her acquaintance would no longer be happy to waltz away alone. He seems reactive: threatening to come undone. The binary star, known collectively as Li Sander, is much more dense and solid than Hel3na, and his materials are extremely volatile. Li Sander can be understood as a pair of superhot burning rocks that combine into a single dazzling source of bright fire.

Gravitational lines criss-cross around them, between them. Hel3na gives them a gentle tug.

Li Sander's twinned rotations stretch out high, changing angle and speed until their connection is so thin it threatens to snap — then draws himself in again. The soft and receptive material of space around him gets dusted with jets of sulphur. A comet sails by, its long tail of ice giving off a faint whistling sound as it tries to go undetected. Hel3na waits for it to pass, then transmits again.

— Hold yourself still, she says.

Li Sander is vibrating with a smaller range than usual, a much tighter orbit. His core is growing hotter and hotter, making the gravity around him creak. He doesn't know how to respond. Hydrogen grains rub together until they blend into helium. Watery stars splash into each other.

— Can you keep secrets?

— Yes.

Hel3na discards part of herself, and presents what's left behind.

— Are you looking?

— So it would seem.

They speak to each other with an intimacy only available to strangers. Li Sander is free to imagine Hel3na stretched out reclining across the blanket — the great gas giant as she was at a particular place in time, a hot rocky centre pulling gaseous strands of smoke in towards her, collecting them and turning them around herself.

Li Sander transfers a single note. Hel3na takes a moment to listen, to interpret the desire behind such an ambiguous frequency. Beneath them both she can hear the deep hum of the galaxy.

Hel3na sends out a pulse. Li Sander detects it, and for

a passing moment the pair of lights stop spinning. Li Sander glows as one star, collecting Hel3na's message. She has sent pink sand and an urgent question.

—   Do you want to see me again like this?

Li Sander twirls around so quickly his two halves come together, a turning spiral galaxy in miniature.

—   Well, he blushes.

And with that, every particle of Hel3na is charged with desires. The background temperature of the universe warms her atoms. Hel3na sends a cloud of purple vapour on a victory lap around her northern hemisphere.

—   Knew it, she whispers, mostly to herself.

The smallest sub-nuclear quiver is stretching the outer limit of space: the most minute tremble begins to change the total shape of the edge.

—   I'm burning up.

—   I should expect you are.

—   And you?

—   That would be telling.

Hel3na understands. A pulse inside an atom at the bottom of one lost corner, tampers with something foreveraway that's otherwise merrily minding its own business. It won't ease up until a wave passes interstellar distances like a flick in a piece of rope. Li Sander doesn't know exactly what's happening, it's just a bump he can feel. A low, dense ripple of intensity that he witnesses Hel3na experiencing also. His orbits are rising and falling beyond his control; she huddles deeper into the fabric of her part of the universe.

Once expressed, a surge of vitality such as this will make itself manifest anywhere it can. There's more than enough to go around as it builds: more over here with me, does not sully how much is fizzing and overflowing, exploding and blooming over there on your end. It gets created — and it's got to go somewhere.

Story of O

'That went well.'

Oberon and Puck were making their way through the forest.

'Welcome the Changeling,' muttered Oberon. He glared at the trees as if they were partly to blame for his troubles. 'And I'm all ready to do that. And then straight off he's getting sent on his merry way. One night indeed!'

A falcon watched from a nearby perch. Oberon stopped and stared sharply at it until it began pecking the branch instead, as if suddenly noticing something very interesting there. Oberon scrunched his hands into his pockets and continued to stalk through the forest as if late for a meeting.

'I just don't see why — and I'm not dismissing Theseus and Hippolyta *personally*, here — but it's clear as a glass raindrop he'll be *wasted* in a mortal court, even a semi-heroic one.'

Puck nodded, trotting along beside him.

Oberon kicked a nut. It clattered against a tree stump. 'I'd put plans in place,' he said, 'I told her I was excited.'

The cypresses made faint swishing sounds as squirrels and brown hares got the hell out of Oberon's way. Puck broke into a light jog to keep up with him.

'We'd all be so well suited.' A breeze swept through the forest, the evening air perfumed with flowers; Oberon frowned at the delightful play of moonlight on speckled leaves and shook his head as if refusing a bottle of cheap wine.

'Not in the mood,' he said.

Puck had started skipping and hopping to avoid the prominent tree roots that were ever more in their path.

Oberon, of course, didn't put a foot wrong. 'Do I make that kind of mistake?' he said. 'Because I don't believe my wont is to make that kind of mistake.'

He marched straight into an area thick with brambles, knowing the thorns wouldn't dare to touch him. Puck received no such special treatment, and some distance grew between them while Puck battled sharp stems thwacking his face and spiked leaves prodding as if asking what the matter was. By the time he emerged from the thorn bush and caught up with Oberon, the King of the Fairies was sitting glumly on a low branch, staring into the soil.

'The wedding will be a disaster,' he said. 'I won't enjoy myself.'

Puck nodded, his silent commiserations going unseen. He pulled another sharp thorn from his sleeve.

'Puck,' said Oberon.

'Yes?' said Puck.

'Answer me honestly.'

'Will do,' said Puck.

Oberon sighed. 'How much have I embarrassed myself?'

Puck hitched himself up onto the branch and sat with his feet dangling. He rested his head against the tenseness of Oberon's shoulder. 'A bit,' he said.

A black bear cub came out from behind the trunk and pottered about in the soil. It pawed the ground, nuzzling at

Oberon's feet.

'I'm not going to feed you,' said Oberon. He was still staring at the ground. 'Perhaps a single night together might not have been so terrible,' he said. 'Did I overreact?'

Puck swung his legs. 'It's understandable, I think. To think things are one way, and then—' he caught a silvery speck of dust in his hand, '—realise you were not quite right.' He blew the dustmote away. 'The problem may have been,' he ventured, 'not the misunderstanding so much, but your stubbornness in the aftermath.'

Oberon finally looked at Puck. The moonlight dappled pleasantly over both of them as if in moral support. From a nearby clearing came the gentle tread of delicate hooves as a pair of roe deer passed by, minding their own business.

'An occasion like tomorrow, we really shouldn't be on bad terms,' said Oberon.

'Could be worse!' said Puck.

Oberon frowned. 'How exactly?'

Puck bobbed up and down as he spoke, making the branch wobble. 'Even if you've gone rattling about and made yourself look a wally,' he said, 'at least you're able to attend the wedding at all — you don't have to miss it because you're accidentally on holiday so you can't go. Because that's what I did! Ha!' He beamed at Oberon. 'Who's the wally now?'

'*What?*' cried Oberon. 'You're not even going to be there?' He covered his face with his hands and slumped further onto the branch. 'This is unbearable.'

Puck tenderly brushed a speck of soil from Oberon's trousers. 'I am sorry, my king,' he said. 'It's true, I got my dates muddled.'

Oberon groaned. Any residual anger had drained away and he felt only sad and cold with missed opportunities. When he closed his eyes he could picture the Changeling taking those steps towards him, remember the warmth of Titania's pleasure at the sight of it.

A scratching sound beside him took his attention. Puck was rummaging around in his satchel. He pulled out a scrappy volume, a collection of loose pieces of parchment tied with string. He presented it towards Oberon's face, open at a page with an inky sprawl.

'It's in the diary, see?' said Puck. 'Holiday.'

Oberon took the diary and examined it. 'Just for my own interest,' he said, 'did you make any preparations for your holiday besides writing it in your own diary?'

Puck shook his head. Oberon gently leafed through a few more pages. All blank. He sighed. 'And there's no way you can move it,' he muttered. He gave Puck his diary back.

'Next time discuss it with me first,' he said, but his voice was flat with futility. Puck nodded and put the tatty volume back inside his satchel.

'In the circumstances,' he said, 'I believe it's even more important the two of you make it up. Ideally tonight.'

'I do wish for that,' said Oberon. 'Let us think of the answer. Together we always do.'

Puck put his hand on his chin, crossed his legs and adopted a *thinking hard* expression he'd seen on a marble statue near the blacksmith's.

'If you went back and apologised,' he offered, 'I'm sure she'd forgive you.'

Oberon shook his head. 'I want to make a grand gesture,' he

said. 'Something with drama.'

'Are you sure?' said Puck. 'I thought you just tried that approach.'

'A dramatic gesture that goes right, this time, and makes her think better of me.'

'Oh I see,' said Puck, 'one of *those*.'

Oberon leant back on the branch and put his feet up, resting one over Puck's knees and letting the other dangle. He felt lighter already. He put his hands behind his head and closed his eyes.

The bear cub wandered off. Puck massaged Oberon's feet, staring into space and thinking.

Oberon opened his eyes and clicked his fingers. 'I've got it! Could you bring me a vial of your moonshine?'

Puck's face lit up. 'Now there's a thought,' he said. He continued to run his hand along the soul of Oberon's foot. 'A gift for them both! Brilliant idea.' He squeezed with his thumb. 'You're quite tight there.'

'If you say so,' said Oberon. Puck grinned and pressed harder, and Oberon groaned in delight.

Puck was a dabbler. He manufactured a substance from a rare flower. He brewed it in copper pans and stored it in old jam jars, safely hidden on the farm where he operated the distillery. It was clear to the touch and lightly sticky, it tingled when it wet the fingers, and it gave a powerful boost to the lusty pleasure of its subject. It was potent stuff, used for special occasions, and the fairies called it Loveliness.

'That should do it!'

'And that's only the beginning of my plan,' said Oberon.

Puck's eyes grew wide as he waited to hear the rest of it.

'I need to show Titania that I wish her well,' said Oberon. 'I can admit that in abandoning them, I have denied her a certain enjoyment, so I will seek to redress the joy she's owed, in absentia. In addition to the Loveliness, I want her to receive a gift of the same qualities she has kindly arranged for others tomorrow.'

Oberon's eyes were sparkling with enthusiasm. His hair had a new shine to it, and his horns were slick and sharp on his temple.

'A new admirer, yes? You're on a roll,' said Puck.

He nodded. 'The Changeling sets a high bar, of course, and given Titania's preferences... we find someone who'll give her what she needs, a real beast, an absolute dreamboat, someone with charisma.'

He frowned a little at the scale of the task and looked off into the trees, thinking hard. This meant he didn't see Puck's face of immediate, passionate revelation.

It was Puck's turn to click his fingers.

Oberon was busy counting on his. 'It must be absolutely the right person,' he muttered. 'Could be him. Or him, that's two. A third idea.... hmm, no, not her — where best to search — many great people arriving into Athens for the wedding — perhaps a warrior is better than a god — but is either better than a poet? It's hard to be sure...'

Puck clicked his fingers a few more times, directly in Oberon's face.

Finally he looked. 'What?'

'Didn't I say to ask me about the thing I saw?'

'When did you say that?'

'Just now,' said Puck, vibrating with excitement, 'moments

ago. With Titania. Right before you did the thing where you made a wally of yourself.'

'I dimly recall,' said Oberon, 'though I was somewhat preoccupied.' Before his mind's eye flashed a beautiful vision of the Changeling. He winced and shook the image away. 'Very well, you clearly want me to, I'll ask now. What did you see?'

Puck took a deep breath in.

'There's a troupe of Athenian tradesfolk rehearsing a play in the forest,' he said. 'And there's one in particular.' Puck grinned triumphantly. 'He's our guy.'

Rhubarb Rhubarb!

In a parched clearing in another part of the forest, new voices sounded.

'... last year's production, during the second — no — the *third* performance,' Starling was saying. 'Snug was supposed to say *good morning* but he actually said — oh, you'd better tell him, Snug.'

Snug spread his arms wide.

'I said *good evening!*'

Starling's laugh rang out through the trees.

Snug's face contorted. He looked about the company. 'Can you believe it?' He smiled at one of their number, a woman in scuffed shoes. 'And you must remember that, Flute?'

'I had no idea what to say!' Flute shook her head in despair. 'I thought poor Snout would have to invent a new speech on the spot.'

'Yes well, I very nearly thought about it,' said Snout in a deep velvet voice. He folded his arms and leaned against a tree trunk, lending his portly stature even more authority than usual. '*Then* where would we have been?' he said.

A pile of scripts lay on a small painter's table. Beside it was a long roller on a pole, and a small scattering of wooden paintbrushes.

'What happened?' asked a politely interested person in faded dungarees. 'How did you get out of it?'

Snug's voice had a note of pride. 'You'll have to ask Quince,' he said. 'She saved us all from impending humiliation.'

Quince was surveying the clearing with her hands on her hips, holding herself poised and ready like a raised baton. She blew a lock of hair from her eyes, where it had momentarily escaped her headscarf.

'I went backstage to the cyclorama,' she explained, 'and cranked the handle at full speed so the sun went down and came up again. After that Snug remembered he was supposed to cue Snout for the Breakfast Maker's Monologue.'

The gathered players rolled about laughing.

The dungarees-wearer laughed politely, joining in. 'That sounds very…' He considered several options before realising he didn't really know. So he smiled at Quince instead, letting the unspecified compliment float away into the air like a balloon.

Quince grinned at Bottom. 'Just one of those things you think of in the moment,' she said.

The players took their scripts from the painter's table. Bottom frowned as he read the title page and unconsciously adjusted the straps of his dungarees, shortening one by an inch or so. The dungarees went wonky on one side, revealing a pleasingly contoured chest.

Behind them, a large sheet hung between two trees. For the moment it was mostly white, barring the odd splotch of housepaint. Eventually it would depict a dramatic backdrop of an interior, carefully painted by Quince. On the ground lay a lumpish hessian bag, bulging with bits of costume, possible props and musical items. Quince strode into the centre of the clearing.

'Right troupe, come gather round,' she said. Her sandals were blotched with paint, which also had gotten onto her toes. She had come directly from work. 'Any questions before we open the bag?'

There was a silence.

'Just a request,' said Snug. 'Please don't give me too many lines.' His hands fluttered in his pocket, tangling his fingers up with a tape measure. He'd left early to get to rehearsal.

Quince the painter grinned at him. 'Understood,' she said.

Snug nodded but he didn't look convinced. 'You're always trying to push me theatrically,' he said. 'I don't mind and I'll try but I'm mostly here for the social aspect.'

'I have a question,' said Starling. 'Am I going to be the love interest?' She removed a small bottle of varnish from a pocket in her skirt and rolled it gently between her fingers.

'I couldn't possibly say,' said Quince, tapping her nose.

'Will I be required to wear a fake beard again?' said Snout, from the back. 'Last time I didn't enjoy the fake beard.'

'It suited you,' said Flute. 'It gave you... what's the word? Gravitas!'

'You're very kind,' said Snout, 'but still. Rather you than me.' He took out a pipe and sparked a light.

Snout looked dapper as ever, and his own grey beard was carefully trimmed. He smelled of whisky and tasteful bergamot cologne, with an undertone of anchovies that nobody minded. He'd come straight from work. They all had.

'We don't stand a chance of bettering your current beard, Snout,' said Quince. 'I wouldn't ask you to change it.'

'What's in the bag then?' demanded Starling the french-polisher. 'If I'm playing my usual sort of character there's probably something thin and delicate in there. We'll have to hang anything like that up before we can use it.'

'Agreed!' added Snug the hosier, unable to overlook such a faux pas. 'Silk crumples very easily.'

'Right — Starling — everyone — you'll find out what's in the bag when we open it,' said Quince. 'That is, if you'll let me.'

'Has anyone learned their lines already?' said Bottom.

'Oh for goodness' sake,' said Quince. 'I'm opening the bag.'

Starling beamed at him. 'Nevermind that, Bottom. I hope we'll get to see your dancing chops.' She sidled over and gave him a pat on the arm. Her gaze drifted slowly down to his feet, a sexual inspection covered by only the thinnest of veneers.

Bottom gently lifted her fingers from his bicep and looked kindly into her eyes. 'I don't know about that,' he said.

'Quince told us you're very good,' said Snout, bringing the pipe to his lips.

'Leave him alone, you two!' Quince was on her knees scrabbling through the bag.

'Feel free to grab items you like the look of,' she said, flinging objects into the clearing. 'Anything that helps get us going.'

The cast were immediately upon various items. Starling found a sea admiral's hat and pressed it onto her head at a coquettish angle. 'What do you think?' she asked Bottom.

'We can definitely use that,' said Quince looking up, still elbow-deep into the bag. 'It's a nautical play.'

'Do you want me to flap some blue fabric about?' said Flute. 'I don't mind, and I had a biggish part last time so it seems fair?' She looked down at her creased blouse and rubbed her thumb against a stain from lunch.

Quince the painter gave her a disapproving look. 'Your talent would be wasted on the blue cloth,' she said. 'In any case, we'll never actually *see* the sea.'

The actors gathered in closer together while Bottom watched politely from the sidelines, his body low in a casual crouch. He removed his hat and scrunched it between his fingers, causing gentle movement in the definition of his muscular arms, and his dungarees slouched to reveal more of his sculptural torso.

Casting a sly glance at all this, Snout the fishmonger puffed on his pipe and raised an eyebrow at Quince.

'Where did you find him again?' he asked, tilting his head towards Bottom.

'At a party,' she said blithely. 'I recognised his talent immediately.'

Flute took a deep breath and approached Bottom, who stood and offered an informal salute. Her gaze hovered timidly at the level of his knees.

'I'm Frances Flute,' she said, 'the plasterer. What was your name again sorry?'

'Bottom,' he said. 'I'm Nick Bottom the tanner.'

Flute nodded.

'Pleased to meet you, Flute,' said Bottom. 'Have you been with the company long?'

Flute's gaze now hung somewhere around Bottom's ankles. 'Oh you know,' she said.

After a brief pause Bottom realised it was once more his turn to speak.

'Um… this will be my first proper acting role,' he said. 'I mean I've performed before but a lot of it is movement-based.'

Bottom was a leatherworker living on the outskirts of

31

Athens. His workshop had a large window through which Athenians sometimes gathered to watch him pounding away with his bare arms and leather apron; it was this that led to initial requests for his talent as a dancer. He was now regularly asked to perform at birthdays, or at the public baths.

Starling came up beside Quince and took her by the elbow, leaning in urgently to whisper.

'This party,' she said, 'where you found Bottom. You said he was dancing?'

Quince suddenly became very interested in the tree-tops. 'Yes, what about it?'

'Just a hunch I have. Was he... wearing clothes?'

Quince shrugged. 'Initially.' She looked at Starling and they shared a brief moment of delirious excitement like children with access to matches.

'*It's my old beard!*' boomed Snout's voice from the direction of the props bag and everyone turned to look. He held up a scrap of threadbare gingerness with an air of fond nostalgia. 'Will it flatter me as much as it used to, do you think?'

Quince and Starling laughed and joined him as he tried the beard on. They beckoned Bottom into the group and he went over, tucking his script into his back pocket.

Flute and Snug found themselves watching quietly from the sidelines. Flute leaned in and whispered to Snug.

'Do you have any idea which part you've got?'

'Not yet,' said Snug. 'It's obvious who the main two will be, though.' They watched their fellow actors with admiration. Starling was playing an Athenian war song on the recorder, teasing Bottom to dance along to it.

Flute nodded. 'Snout and Starling are both brilliant,' she said.

'And Quince,' added Snug.

'Come on you two,' Quince held a paintbrush towards them like a ready sword. 'I'm not letting Flute and Snug miss out on the fun!'

Snug went over to shake Bottom by the hand.

'Pleased to meet you,' he said. 'I'm Snug the hosier.'

'Hello, Snug,' said Bottom. 'I know your shop.'

Snug went the colour of Snout's pretend beard. 'Well that's nice,' he said. 'Now we're in the same acting troupe I can do you Artist's Discount.' He beamed widely.

'That's so nice of you,' said Bottom. 'That's really kind!' Bottom squeezed Snug's hand a final time and finished the handshake, since Snug seemed happy to keep it going.

Quince was delighted to see everyone in the company getting along so well. She considered herself, fundamentally, to be a people person; she brought others together to conjure a reality from a dream. Her gaze fixed upon Bottom's jawline...

She ran a hand over her head, disrupting the scarf. She untied it and went to refasten the fabric, before deciding against and letting her hair tumble loose instead.

'Prefer it down actually...' she muttered. She dropped the scarf to the ground and addressed the company.

'Right then,' she said. 'Would everyone like to learn who they are in this play?'

There was a chorus of affirmatives and everyone made themselves comfortable. Snout sat on a tree stump. Flute remained standing by the bushes. Starling lowered herself onto a bendy branch and crossed her legs as if she sat on an elegant chair. Snug knelt on the floor. Bottom lowered himself to the ground and flung his arms casually over his knees. Snug glanced

33

towards Bottom, then slowly slid his legs out from under him until he too was sitting that way.

Quince cleared her throat. 'You all know the play,' she said. 'Theseus asked for a wedding-day performance that would showcase the greatness of Athenian drama.' She raised her script triumphantly. 'I thought this fit the bill nicely.'

'It's the perfect text,' said Snout, 'and ambitious too!'

'I'm glad you think so,' agreed Quince. 'We need to tackle it with all the confidence we have.'

Bottom knew he was being stared at. He could feel various pairs of eyes but when he looked everyone happened to be staring intensely at Quince. He smiled to himself — people were often like this at the baths, too. He concentrated his attention on Quince as well.

'I've thought very hard about the casting of this piece,' she said. 'This is an important performance, it has to be right. And do you know what? I think, with everyone we've got here, it will be.' She looked warmly at the company, and gave ceremonial light to Snout.

'Snout: I'd like you to play Pyramus.'

'It would be an honour.' Snout's deep voice was rich with pride. He smiled and drew a circle around the word *Pyramus* in the list of characters at the beginning of his script.

'Pyramus is a good part, one of the best in the play,' said Quince, as the company whispered *congratulations* and *well dones* in his direction. 'It's got tragedy, pathos, a nice bit of disgrace and redemption at the end… let's aim for tears.'

Snout was going through the script drawing yellow marks under the Pyramus lines. He nodded, excitedly.

Quince turned to Flute. 'You're Thisbe.'

Flute's face fell open with shock. She looked as if she hadn't even known a casting was happening. Starling rubbed her back and whispered, 'Congratulations Flute, that's fantastic!'

Flute composed herself a little. 'I can't believe it.'

Quince nodded. 'It's another tragic role of course; supporting Pyramus, but with your own height to fall from. I think you'll bring a certain vulnerability. And where it matters,' she added, with affection that went back years, 'you can get a laugh. I've seen you.'

Quince winked at Flute. Snout gave her a thumbs-up, still holding the pen.

'You can borrow this when I've done with it,' he said.

Flute beamed. 'Thanks!'

Quince the painter looked back at the script. 'I think the best way to demonstrate your part, Snug, is to show you the costume.'

From the hessian bag she pulled forth a floppy tail, fashioned from soft felt in yellow and orange, and a headpiece upon which were sewn two large pointed ears. One folded over itself adorably.

'We'll make a mane for you as well,' said Quince. 'And before you start, it's an important part, but you'll be glad to know you don't have that many lines.'

She turned to Bottom.

Bottom was still sitting in the centre of the clearing, gently holding onto his ankles. The others had unconsciously formed a circle around him.

A smile played about Quince's face, the *you'll want to thank me in a moment* smile usually reserved for announcing that a buffet is open.

'Bottom.'

'Yes?'

'Willy.'

Starling gasped.

'That's right,' said Quince. 'Our lead role — Willy Loman!'

Flute and Snug beamed. Snout looked up from his script in pleasant surprise, his hand partially obscuring the title of the play: *Death of a S...*

'Of course!' said Starling. 'That's just about the perfect casting, Quince.'

Bottom took it all in his stride. 'Nice,' he said.

Delight in the House of Titania

'Now *this* one is beautiful!'

Titania picked out a piece of silk from the wooden chest and held it aloft, spreading it between her hands. From the chest spilled further bolts of silk in a range of precious sheens. The Changeling was performing chin-ups from a solid branch.

He spoke between breaths as he lifted his bodyweight.

'That was.

'My favourite.

'As well.'

Titania let the silk run smoothly through her fingers. 'The detailing though,' she said in disbelief. 'Look at the life in the stitching. I'd swear these peacocks are vibrating their tails at me.'

She watched as the Changeling performed a final lift, holding his body out horizontally from the branch before dropping neatly to the ground.

Titania looked again at the silks draped over her hands. 'I can't decide,' she said. 'They'd all be perfect for tomorrow.'

'It's no surprise! My city makes the best silks in the world and now you've got one of each.'

'It's an incredibly generous gift. You know you didn't need to.'

Keeping his arms outstretched the Changeling bent over and touched his toes. 'I wanted you to be reminded of my appreciation.'

'I will be. It's very kind of you.'

'And it will be an honour for me if you're wearing any.' He looked at her. 'Isn't it first rate, how they all show you off equally?'

An excited hum spread across her body, pushing against her ribcage. 'Come here, flatterer,' she said. With a final sigh she poured the silks back into the chest.

He sat down beside her, cross-legged. She looked at him.

'I'm ready,' he said.

The moon was already visible in the sky.

'Go on then,' said Titania, initiating things. 'Show me what you Changelings can do.'

He walked to the centre of the clearing, the other fairies turning eagerly to watch. Titania observed how his shoulders adjusted with his confident gait. The Changeling closed his eyes and stretched out his arms. They all followed his movements, sitting bolt upright — and as he centered himself, a new feeling flowed over them.

He opened his eyes and smiled at Titania, and his happiness was a white light that now seemed to surround him, pulsing gently and sending a glow across the forest. The Changeling stood there with a full erection.

'Now that's what I'm talking about,' said Titania.

All the hours they'd waited melted into the single moment as she allowed his energy to envelop her, basking in the full beam of his talents. He was concentrating with extreme calm — an air that made the heat run to her cheeks.

She drifted purposefully towards him and placed her hands around his neck, letting the texture of her dress gently pull across the eager tip of him, prolonging the tease of it while she scrunched her fingers into his hair and gently tugged; his head angled back a little while he kept the cast of his eyes upon her.

The dust in the air was gliding around them in the dim light. A quiet heat was rolling over the ground, curling up the leaves and turning the lint on the topsoil.

His tongue gently met hers.

The glow around them swelled. She felt the building of pressure, and the heat of his body against her chest.

He tilted his head to kiss down the side of her neck, and Titania arched herself and closed her eyes, letting her dress fall to her arms, her body seeking the clasp of his hands. All focus, he acted to her needs. She felt a bolt as his hands worked with expert understanding, and she shivered under his touch. She heard his breath catch.

Titania pushed her thumbs into the tissue of his taut arm muscle: he ran his hands down her, leisurely dragging his index finger across the slope from her hips to her thighs, bringing further heat where she was already hot. Blood rushed downwards, circling inside her, making her dizzy.

In her imagination she conjured the outline of Oberon standing beside them, and felt a flash of melancholy that he wasn't. She firmly pushed herself against him.

They rubbed against each other with steady movement, becoming more rapid and heavy, his face full of concentration. Her fingers were kneading into the muscle of his behind.

The moss grew softer beneath their feet. She could feel a steady beat over her legs. She let her dress fully drop away.

The Changeling buzzed at the sight of her before him, and he pulled her closer in towards his body, his fingers able to touch her with a new intimacy.

Together they lowered themselves to the ground.

He lay on his back, reaching up to run his hands over Titania's stomach as she placed herself on top of him. She put a hand down behind her, parting to guide him in; it happened with giving ease. She took a quick breath in at her fullness, moving a little to acquaint herself with the sense of it. From above him, she observed the Changeling looking up at her.

Titania began to rock.

He was focused, staring calmly straight ahead into her eyes, thrusting with regular breaths and economy of movement. Titania ground herself over him, jolting her hips, making their skin roll tightly together under her weight.

She raised her head to take in the bright and round moon above them, straddling the shape of his torso, revelling in the complementing double of his soft skin under her hands and the roughness between her thighs.

The ground was absorbing the Changeling's white glow as the light started to bend. As her orgasm began to roll up, forming and breaking and steady, she looked down at the Changeling and changed the pace of her thrusts. He understood and immediately followed. Her body opened and she widened her mouth.

There. They gasped together as Titania burst through and into it, and the Changeling's definitive thrusts gave a rock to her giddy senses; as at once his body and hers rang out in concert.

The wave went powering over and through. Her movements let loose as she was grinding over the Changeling and she ramped in her rhythm, her precision falling apart, sailing through — she came down towards him, her pleasure disintegrating into an uncountable number of grains blowing out across the wind, and his arms were wrapped tightly over her body, holding her there, and they lay, breathing together, in no rush to recover.

There was stillness.

A troupe of fireflies went through the clearing in perfect formation like a low-flying meteor shower.

Titania lay with heavy eyelids and one arm flung above her head. The Changeling sat beside her, gliding his fingers through her hair. He leaned over and gave her a light kiss on her mouth, and she responded approvingly to his lips. He looked back up into the sky, which by now was an open cosmos, loaded with stars, winking at him. He nodded to himself, once, with not a little pride and a whole lot of purpose.

In silence, as she fell into sleep, he gently left her side. He picked up his backpack and slung it over his shoulders, then knelt to lace up a pair of white running shoes. He stood, reached out to a low-hanging fig, picked it, munched into it, then set off at a light jog into the trees. The rustling of his movements gradually faded; but not before they were heard by Oberon, who arrived into the clearing moments after the Changeling left.

Oberon was aware of the absence around him. He looked around the bower, a feeling of anguish tugging at him the way Puck sometimes pulled expectantly at his sleeves.

'Missed it.'

He tiptoed around the fairies who lay sleeping in naked heaps.

He knew where she was; he bent a little to dip between the boughs. The trees caught some silver from the full moon above and Titania was bathed in its gentle dappled light.

Her dress lay beside her, thin and unclasped like the boundary between the hours, and she lay uncovered in the warmth of the night on her new bed of moss.

He knelt next to her. She rolled onto her side so she was facing him, her hair spread about her shoulders and neck, still wet with sweat near her hairline.

'Evening,' he whispered. 'Don't mind me.' A new breeze swept across them, bringing the sugary scent of fresh peaches and figs.

Oberon reached into the pocket of his cloak and brought out a small vial. The liquid glowed inside the thick glass. He looked at it for a moment, tipping it this way and that in his hand.

Titania made a tiny noise in her sleep. A smile played over her face, softening the shape of her lips.

'May I put this on you?' said Oberon.

With a deep breath Titania turned to lie on her other side, facing away from him and said in a quiet voice: '*Get about it, then.*' Oberon's gaze followed the slope of her back, and his heart hurt.

'You were right in arranging things this way,' he admitted. 'Of course you were.'

With a deft movement he pulled the cork from the the vial and held it at an angle over his hand. The thick liquid took a few seconds to pour slowly over his fingers.

He inched closer and with his other hand stroked her shoulders, tracing his fingers from the nape of her neck all the way down her back. His fingers moved steadily down towards the bare bottom of the Queen of the Fairies.

Titania took a quick breath in as the tingling liquid made contact with her skin. Oberon moved his hand down until his fingers stroked between her buttocks, and he gently coated her with the liquid. Finally he put in the tip of his finger, then removed it, brushing the remainder of the Loveliness onto his thigh.

Pleased at having delivered, Oberon stood. He dropped the glass vial into his pocket and went away into the trees. As he passed, the peach tree doubled its load.

And in her sleep Titania began, very slowly, to move. She moved her legs, still lying on her side, rubbing her thighs together as she breathed deeply; her exhalations were long and slow. Soon her breathing was audible across the bower.

The moon overflowed and the whole forest breathed deeply in time with Titania. She ran her hands over her body and curled over; she put a finger in her mouth to gently bite it.

Finally she rolled onto her back, and with a sudden rush she gasped as if newly emerged from a pool of icy water. The universe shuddered with her desire; she opened her eyes dazzled by the blaze.

'Ok,' said Titania. 'Wow.'

BLOCKING

'Let's run it again, through to the bit where Bottom comes in.'

Snout put his script down and rubbed his face. 'It's going well, I think,' he said. 'Quite intense, isn't it? I like all these desperate looks we're sharing.'

Flute nodded. 'I can feel there's a long-buried rivalry between us,' she said.

Snout, Flute and Quince were in the clearing, sitting around a plasterer's workbench that had been erected to stand in for a kitchen table. Near the edge of the cleaning, leaning against the papery white trunk of a birch tree, stood a painting roller on the end of a six-foot pole, which for the purposes of rehearsal the cast were pretending was a sports trophy. Snout in particular kept looking at the roller, understanding how the trophy haunted his character. An empty chair was sitting at the head of the table.

The burning moon was getting higher, reworking the shadows as nightfall ripened.

Snug and Starling, who did not have much to do in the scene, sat on a low horizontal branch being the audience.

'That was great, by the way,' said Starling. 'Quince, I loved your bit about not being able to get the clay oven fixed.'

Quince used a pencil to put a small tick mark by one of her

speeches. 'Thank you!' she said. 'I was aiming for somewhere between anguish and crushing defeat.'

She stood from her chair, rising neatly from player to director. 'Ready for your entrance, Bottom?' she called.

Bottom stuck his head through the foliage. 'Not really?'

He stood at the edge of the playing area waiting for his cue. His hands made nervous movements across his dungarees.

'You can do it, Bottom!' called Snug from the branch, sympathetically.

Quince left the kitchen table and went over to him.

'It's normal to feel nervous,' she said, placing her hand on his arm. 'But don't worry. Nobody is judging you — except positively for giving it a go! If anything doesn't feel right we can work out why and try again. That's why we call ourselves mechanicals — it's not all spur-of-the-moment. It's a system you learn, and we're a well-oiled machine.' She smiled up at him encouragingly. 'Okay?'

Bottom took a leap of trust. 'I'm sure I'll get into it once I've started,' he said. He looked at his script.

'You're very tired. Your character travels the land trying to make sails, and it's proving more difficult each day.'

Bottom nodded. 'And on top of that, the sailsman is disappointed in his sons Pyramus and Thisbe, because they haven't amounted to much.'

'That's right. He's dejected, exhausted, he worries his life is meaningless.'

'Right,' said Bottom. He put the script in his back pocket. 'So I'll come in and see if I can get any of that across.'

'That's the spirit,' said Quince. She returned to the kitchen — stepping neatly between the piles of twigs that marked the door — and, immediately in character, spoke urgently to Snout and Flute.

'Don't you know that your father is struggling?' she said. 'Nobody is interested in his sails any more!'

'Not even the philosophers of Thrace?' said Snout. 'They gotta be buyin' surely.' He adjusted in his chair. 'They love Pop, don't they?'

'The librarians of Knossos all know his name,' added Flute.

'You think the love of a philosopher gets you far in this world?' cried Quince. 'That having respect among librarians means anything when you're at the market?' Her voice grew low and serious. 'Do you know what I found in your father's chariot the other day?'

On the far edge of the clearing stood Bottom, holding a wooden crate filled with paintbrushes, mouthing his opening lines to himself.

Flute banged her fist onto the table. 'Tell us Mom, for gods' sake! What did you find?'

'A whittling knife,' said Quince, 'to cut the wheel spokes.'

Flute and Snout gaped at Quince. She looked at them accusingly.

'Yes, that's right: your father wants to kill himself. That's how bad it's gotten for him, and it's all because of you two!' She pointed at Snout. 'Especially you. He thought you would amount to something great, but you haven't.'

Snout and Flute looked at each other, stupefied.

Bottom had picked up the crate too soon. He put it down again.

'It can't be true,' said Snout desperately. 'He coulda gotten the knife for fixin' the chariot if the axle breaks, or—'

'If you don't believe it, you aren't looking hard enough at what he's going through,' said Quince. 'Every night he walks through that door a broken man.'

Bottom took a deep breath, picked up the crate and carried it across the threshold of the playing area. He paused outside the entrance to the kitchen, put the crate down and leaned backwards, pressing his hands onto the small of his back.

'Oh boy oh boy,' he said.

He performed an exaggerated waddle into the kitchen.

Quince rose from the table. Snout and Flute looked at each other, as if worried their conversation had been overheard.

'Here's your father home,' chattered Quince brightly. 'You're a little early, dear.'

Bottom glared at Quince as if such things were none of her business. She sat again at the table, and mimed pouring a glass of water from a jug.

Bottom looked blankly into space for a moment. Then he removed his script from his pocket and opened it. He read over the page to make sure he had the right passage, then took a deep breath to deliver his line.

'O!' he said.

'Very good,' said Quince, quietly.

'What a tiresome day I've had,' said Bottom. 'I am so very tired. I didn't get further than Thebes. Why is that? There were days I used to go all the way out to Corinth and Sparta. But today I turned the chariot around right outside Thebes. I just couldn't do it. I sat there, reins in my hand, thinking: who am I?'

'You're Willy Loman, a renowned sailsman of Athens,' encouraged Quince. Snout and Flute nodded eagerly.

Bottom shrugged. 'I guess,' he said. He turned a page of the script. 'That's who I am,' he added.

On the branch, Snug and Starling shared an impressed look between themselves.

'I'm worried about my love scene with Bottom,' whispered Starling. 'What if I'm not seductive enough?'

'You'll be wonderful,' said Snug. 'Between the two of you there's bound to be phenomenal chemistry. When are you putting the negligee on?'

'Not for ages. Our scene together isn't until the final act. You'll have done your whole bit before I'm wearing the nighty.'

They faced the clearing and continued to watch their fellow actors with admiration. They didn't notice a small shower of cashew shells landing on the ground beside them.

'Did you make many sails today darling?' asked Quince.

Bottom sighed desperately and looked at the ground. Snout and Flute shared a look of concern over the kitchen table.

'Nobody wanted a sail,' muttered Bottom. 'I didn't make a single sail. It keeps happening. All the docks and all the ports, everywhere I go, everyone says they don't need sails.' Bottom sat down at the table. 'Even our returning fleets aren't interested. I don't know what I'm doing wrong.'

Quince went to stand behind Bottom. She rubbed his back, leaning forward slightly to read his script over his shoulder. 'It's only a dry spell, Willy. It will pass. You'll soon make plenty of sails again. I know it for sure.'

High in the tree — above Snug and Starling — Puck was lounging about among the tallest branches as if he occupied a private opera box. He leaned back with his feet up in front of him, munching on honey-roasted cashew nuts from a paper bag.

'You learn some things about yourself, working in sails,'

mumbled Bottom.

Puck put two fingers in his mouth and whistled. He clapped his hands and another shower of cashew shells clattered through the branches, bouncing lightly on the moss.

'More!' shouted Puck. The actors below didn't hear him.

Snout reached out towards Bottom. 'You'll make a huge sail soon, Pop. Maybe for a great galleon or a warship. You're still the best sailsman in Athens!'

Bottom flung himself away from Quince and marched with vigour to the far side of the kitchen. In the tree Puck leaned out between the boughs, his head poking through the leaves.

'Oh yes,' said Puck. 'Yes indeedy.'

Bottom pointed at Snout.

'Maybe I wouldn't have to be,' he said, 'if you and your brother went out and learned an honest trade.' His eyes screwed up as the anger grew. 'I always thought you'd amount to something but I come home and every day you haven't amounted to much.'

He turned another page of his script, wincing slightly at the sight of a large block of text. 'Let me tell you something,' he said, with a note of reluctance.

'What's wrong, Pop?' said Flute.

High in the tree Puck wiggled his fingers, ever so slightly. It was time to make some adjustments.

'You're a disappointment to me, both of you,' began Bottom — and he immediately felt different. Something about him was growing bigger.

'Each day I wonder if one of you will make me proud,' he said, 'but you actually make me mad.' With Puck's assistance some physical changes were coming over Bottom, and as he shook his head his jaw and chin took on longer shadows in the dimming light.

'Dammit Thisbe! Can't you get through to your brother?' cried Bottom, his voice rising, ringing out through the clearing. He paced to the other side of the kitchen, gesturing angrily towards the useless clay oven. He went to the birch tree and placed his hand on the paint-roller, frowning at it in contemplation.

Puck beamed and wiggled his fingers at Bottom, a little more this time.

Bottom felt something flowing through him like newly-lit fire. The script crumpled between his fingers as he screwed it to a tight ball — he found he knew the words. He turned back to face the table.

'Remember when you were a young man, Pyramus, and you won the athletics match?' His voice cracked with desperate nostalgia. 'Gold in the discus! Bronze in the slingshot! Twice gold in close combat, for crying out loud! I look at this trophy every day. Pyramus, you could've been an Olympian! Why'd you give up on yourself?'

Bottom lifted his arms in exasperation, and the straps of his dungarees split for good. The garment fell to his waist, baring his muscular chest that rippled with every great breath that he took, and thanks to Puck, his upper body was covered with a fine down of brown fur.

Puck laughed and clapped his hands in delight, before pointing once more into the centre of the clearing.

'You're gorgeous,' said Puck. 'I can't stop!'

Bottom seethed with a new vitality. He found himself enjoying a surge of confidence in his words. He looked around the

51

clearing and saw, like a ghost overlaying the forest trees, the family's derelict villa: the faded and peeling fresco on the kitchen walls; the rickety chariot in the yard; the mosaic tiles, now cracked and covered with mould, around the steam bath they'd once been so proud of.

He whipped his tail against the back of his thigh.

His hefty ears swivelled around, newly increased in sensitivity and length. He huffed a breath through his nose and flicked his thick, powerful tongue over full lips.

'Don't you want to be the best version of yourself?' he bellowed, pawing the ground with his leg, leaving deep impressions in the soil.

Puck threw him a wink, making finger guns. Bottom took great strides back across the kitchen, feeling the gait of his muscular thighs and the heaviness of his newly thick cock hanging between his legs.

The words were flowing through him. Bottom bowed his head and the architecture of his neck changed to support the weight. His fur bristled along the contours of his shoulders and arms. He ran a hand across his jaw and looked around the Loman family kitchen with glistening green eyes.

High in the tree, Puck placed a hand either side of his face, bathing in the vision of the beast in the moonlight. His development of Bottom was complete. 'You'll do!' he said.

Bottom pressed his hands onto the kitchen table and leaned into it.

'Instead of giving up on yourself, you should hold it down and get up and then you might amount to something and stop amounting to nothing!' he cried. 'Can't you be something?'

He paused. Snout and Flute were staring at him in horror.

Flute's mouth was moving but no words were coming out. Quince began backing away from the table.

Bottom was breathing deeply. He moved his hand across his forehead, noticing the thickness of his fingernails. He leaned his weight once more into the table and felt it creak with the pressure. His breath was all power, as if he had just won a race.

Bottom tried his line again. 'Can't you be something?'

He flashed a look to where Quince had been. He began to ask 'Isn't it Snout's line?' but there was a sharp crack over his ear as he was hit from behind, and the dizzy sting of a blunt object landed flat across the side of his face.

He looked around in confusion, an aching burn already spreading through his neck, and the object hit him again over his ribs. He staggered sideways.

Bottom's attackers kept back in the shadows.

He was hit across the ribs once more, and he fell.

On the ground the stick smacked his body, hard into his hip-bone. He curled onto his side.

A foot kicked him hard into the back of his thigh. He moaned and curled further in on himself, tightening as much as he could to protect his organs. He felt the movement of the stick rising again. His body lay there in the soil, tight in a flinch, his eyes squeezed closed. It smacked hard across his shoulder, catching his face. There was a crunch in his neck, a sudden ringing in his ear.

The stick broke. The halves of the paint-roller were taken up and turned into two truncheons. One strike quickly followed another. Bottom clasped his hands around his head and rolled over onto his front, his face down. A blow came down hard over his back. Another hit his hand. He heard the sharp crack of his fingers breaking. He opened his mouth in a silent scream towards the soil.

Bottom recoiled from the kicks. He curled his tail around his body. His broken hand dropped from his face, and rolling his eyes he could make out figures advancing, retreating, raising their legs to kick again. He lay against the darkness of the earth, his face pressed into the black soil: the acid nausea; the blood and dirt in his mouth; the snapping agony from his twisted hand.

A smudge of cloud hung scattered and thin overhead.

Bottom lay there limp in the centre of the clearing.

The two halves of the paint roller dropped to the floor.

Bottom was an indistinct shape on the ground. Quince, Snout, Flute, Snug and Starling moved silently until they disappeared into the forest.

After the Mechanicals

The tree shook as Puck timidly lowered himself down. For a moment he crouched on the lowest branch, peering out into the darkness. Then with a swift jump he left the tree and landed on the ground. The cashew shells were mixed up in the soil.

Puck took a deep breath. He ran a hand across his eyes. The black shape in the centre of the clearing wasn't moving.

His hand remained frozen over his face for a moment. Then he walked quickly towards Bottom's body and stood over it.

Bottom lay curled over onto his side. Puck crouched to take a closer look at his face. The eyes were closed; one was already swollen. His lips were parted and blood had started to become dark and hardened where the blows had hit him.

Puck delicately placed a hand on Bottom's shoulder, looking him over. Bruising was already visible and the fur was matted with blood in places. The fingers of one hand lay loosely, at an odd angle.

Standing again, Puck looked around the dark clearing. The forest stared back at him in silence.

Puck chewed on his lip. From the back of his throat he let out the smallest sound of panic.

He hurried around to Bottom's large back and gave him a push. The weight pushed back against him. Puck shook his head, screwing up his eyes and mouthing unspoken words. Then he turned around, pressed his own back against Bottom's body and pushed again, his knees folded in front of him and his teeth bared with the effort. Bottom didn't move. Puck gave up the push and stayed there a moment, wheezing. He lay his head against Bottom's fur, then noticed Bottom's tail slowly drag itself into a curl. He went to examine it.

The tail hadn't been damaged. He gently stroked the tuft of fur at the end and considered his options.

He moved until he was kneeling beside Bottom's head. He put his hands underneath the shoulders and heaved. Bottom didn't move. Puck pulled again, leaning backwards with the effort. This time Bottom's head and shoulders lifted slightly from the mud. Then Puck's strength was spent and Bottom flopped back down.

'Okay,' said Puck.

He wrapped his arms around Bottom's body and hoisted until Bottom was sat roughly upright. Then he crawled forwards until he was squatting close, feeling the warmth of Bottom's chest leaning onto him. He took Bottom's arm, being careful not to touch the wrongly bent fingers, and slung it over his shoulder, shuffling around until he was crouched with Bottom's weight pressing heavily onto his back. Then he heaved.

Slowly Puck stood, unfolding himself until he took Bottom's entire weight.

He performed a quick shrug forwards and Bottom hung across his shoulders like an oversized fur stole. His tail brushed against the back of Puck's knees.

Puck stood there a moment, trembling under the weight.

'Now I do this,' he said. 'Get it together, Puck.' He raised a foot and began a slow forward motion.

Craning his neck and concentrating, Puck could feel a low pulse from a place far away in the forest and he headed there, making a papery tread over old leaves.

Puck and Bottom made their unsteady way forward. Puck's eyes were fixed firmly into the distance. Sweat trickled down the side of his face, which was set in an eerie grimace from the overbearing weight over his shoulders and back. The forest blurred around him.

*

After some time he staggered into the area marked by the gnarled and ancient fig tree. Puck pressed his head into the weight above him in an attempt to raise his sightline.

There was a movement nearby.

'Who's there?' came a voice.

At the sound of Blossom's call, Puck finally released the lumbersome weight from his shoulders. The body slid to the ground with a thud.

The sight stopped Blossom in her tracks. 'Puck?'

She looked at the bloody form at Puck's feet. 'What happened here?' she said. 'What have you found?'

Puck was wobbling slightly on the spot.

Hurrying over, Spidersilk joined them and knelt beside the dark shape on the floor. Immediately she raised her head and called out, her voice spinning through the trees.

'Hey!' she said. 'There's been an accident. I think it's one of us.'

There was movement around the forest as the fairies woke and came swiftly to where they were needed. Holding hands, Mustardseed and Buttermilk arrived first, and soon Bottom was surrounded by cautious figures, moving in closer. Puck slowly stepped backwards out of the gathering.

Blossom reached out a friendly hand and rested it on his shoulder.

'Do you know him?' she said.

Puck's eyes were glazed, oblivious to the question.

She tried again. 'Where did you find this...?'

'... somewhere over in the wood,' said Puck in a small voice. He was trembling beneath Blossom's hand.

'Well, you've done a good deed,' said Blossom.

Puck turned and looked intensely at her. 'Are you sure I did?'

Blossom frowned. 'Of course,' she said. 'By the look of things, this is the best place for him. If he belongs anywhere it's with us.'

The body on the ground was surrounded by featherlight motion. The fairies were assessing the damage, conferring between themselves.

Blossom gave Puck's shoulder a small squeeze. 'Hey,' she said. 'That must have been really tough to do alone. I'm sorry. But you could well have saved him.'

'Shouldn't have needed saving!' Puck turned and ran off into the trees. Blossom watched him go, following the small figure until he had vanished.

The fairies had finished examining him.

'Does anyone recognise who this is?' Blossom asked as she

joined them. 'I'm not sure Puck knew how he came to be here.'

There were various murmurs from the fairies. Mustardseed shook his head.

'None of us have seen him before,' said Lingus.

The fairies spaced themselves until they surrounded Bottom, bent down and placed their hands beneath him. Heaving together they lifted him slowly from the floor, and with steady steps carried him towards the fig tree.

The fairie Lilly was holding one of Bottom's big legs. 'Could he be another Changeling?' she asked.

'Titania would have told us.' Fuchsia was walking carefully backwards, supporting the weight from his battered shoulder. She carefully adjusted her fingers over the fur.

'He is familiar…' muttered Buttermilk.

They carried Bottom a little further in silence.

'We should tell Titania straight away,' said Lilly. 'She'll want to know.'

Blossom shook her head. 'We should fix him first.'

The fairies adjusted their grip on his body, keeping him steady as they maneuvered over the prominent tree roots.

'Well, we can all see what's happened,' said Lingus, looking over Bottom's black eye.

Mustardseed nodded. 'I wonder if he'll remember.'

'I hope not,' said Spidersilk.

They came close to the outermost branches of the giant fig tree, still holding Bottom between them.

Lullaby stopped. 'Let's put him here.'

Warm air passed over the forest and Bottom's mouth opened in a silent gasp.

Bottom landed softly down.

*

He opened his eyes. With a groan he squeezed them closed. Then he opened them again, slower this time, and moved his head a little, looking around with bleary confusion. His eyes widened at the sight of the beautiful being who knelt beside him.

'My name is Lullaby,' she smiled. 'You might find you still ache a bit.'

Around him stood a troupe of lithe bodies, looking at him with fascination and excitement. Some were wearing flowers or silk, many wore nothing at all.

Bottom rubbed his eyes with his knuckles. It felt good, releasing him from an itch deep down. He carried on rubbing his eyes. Then with a sudden move he held his hand away from his face and looked at it, spreading out his fingers.

The brown fur was sleek and soft again. Bottom wiggled his fingers. They were stiff, but working fine.

The throng moved backwards a little as Bottom sat up and gingerly ran his hands over himself. There was no longer any swelling around his eyes. His jaw was firm and in perfect shape. He carried on feeling around, paying new attention to his insides. His chest was moving seamlessly with the rhythm of his breathing. And he was conscious of a new feeling thrumming across his body, strong and vibrant. He licked his unbroken hand with his large pink tongue.

On the floor were his dungarees, newly clean and neatly folded. Bottom realised he was naked, his legs splayed over the moss.

'We had to undress you for it to work,' said Lullaby.

'Honest,' said one of the others.

A new voice spoke, full of warmth and sweet as honey. 'What wonderful thing just happened here?'

Emerging from beneath the fig tree, pushing aside the heavily laden branches, was a new figure wearing a garment of flowers. Her hair tumbled loose, flowing behind her as she came towards him.

'He was in a bad state,' said Lullaby, 'and we mended him. We don't know who he is.'

Bottom looked at the impressive figure before him, and the mostly naked group that framed her.

'Is he a Changeling?' asked one of them.

She knelt by his side and placed a hand on his chest, pressing her fingers into the softness of his fur. 'Something like that,' she said. 'But not until recently. This body has been newly made.' She gazed at his face for a long moment. 'You're clever too, to have known to find me. What are you about then, unique creature?'

Bottom's eyes grew wide, and his mouth opened accidentally.

'Very good. You're going to be fine.' Standing she held a hand towards him. Bottom raised himself to his feet. Inside his belly all sorts of things were fluttering about.

'Come with me,' she said.

The group parted to let them through. Lullaby caught Bottom's eye with a bright smile as he passed and gave him a thumbs-up.

Bottom let himself be led beneath the fig tree, intoxicated with the sense of the unknown.

He was surrounded by branches holding on to thick leaves. An oil lamp hung above, spilling warm light over everything.

Beside him was a small bowl filled with apricots, a jug of water flavoured with orange blossoms, and two glasses.

'Make yourself comfortable,' she said, gesturing about the space.

He gave himself a firm scratch between his ears. Noticing how her eyes followed the movement, he offered a subtle flex of his arms. He settled down onto a soft patch of earth.

She came to sit opposite him, looking at him intensely. A sudden delightful tingle told her the Loveliness was working. Her fingers drew Bottom's gaze as they stroked loosely over her collarbone.

'Well isn't it something, you wandering about in my neck of the woods,' she said. 'You look gorgeous like that, by the way.'

Bottom melted.

'You're through the toilsome part. It's lots of fun from here on in.' Her eyes looked straight into his. Her full attention washed over him. 'What happened to you?'

He lowered his eyes, noticing the glossy down over his body, covering his chest and belly, leading to a thicker patch of fur at the base of his cock. He looked up into her eyes again and felt a rush of heat.

'I don't know,' he said. 'I think I — I do remember I damaged my hand.' He held it out.

'Oh, I'm not asking about the injuries,' she said. 'It's obvious what happened to you *there*, we can put that behind us. What I want to know about is—' Her eyes performed a split-second flick from the tips of his ears to his crotch, straight back into his eyes. 'All *this* delightful business. Can you remember where it came from?'

'Oh.' Bottom looked again at his hands, and the brown fur

that sloped down the muscles of his arms. 'I think this, just, sort of *happened*.'

'I see,' she said, telling the truth. 'Well, I might take it upon myself to look after you for now; I'm good at that sort of thing. My name is Titania,' she added, looking into his face again. 'I'm Queen of the Fairies. Nice to meet you.'

Bottom felt his cock stirring. He ran a hand over his jaw and down again over his chest, and carefully sat up a little further. 'I'm Bottom the tanner,' he said, and he thought he should add something. 'I live in Athens and I work in leather.'

'*Do* you now,' said Titania. Her next breath had a quiver to it — and across the forest, arid grasses flicked taut in unison. 'I imagine that must be difficult work?'

Bottom slowly moved his hand in a *so-so* gesture. 'It's quite physical but I enjoy it.' He thought for a moment. 'It's stretchy.'

Titania leaned forwards to the water jug and filled their glasses. 'Lots of hammering I expect, and heavy lifting. But it must need a delicate touch — do you also sew and mend?'

'Oh yes. As a matter of fact I make my own costumes.'

Titania picked up one of the glasses. 'What are the costumes for?'

'I'm a dancer.'

'A dancer?'

'Yes. For private parties and things.'

Titania's glass remained halfway to her mouth.

Bottom grinned. His erection was hard and proud now. He straightened his arms, sitting up higher and pushing out his powerful chest.

Titania held a glass out to him. 'So that's what you do with yourself out of hours?'

'Yes.' Bottom took the glass.

'Well lucky me,' said Titania. 'It's late enough; perhaps when you feel ready you'll show me a little something?'

She clinked her glass against his and they drank together, eyed locked. Bottom's body was pulsing to a strange new rhythm, as if he were dancing already.

FARMYARD

A cat was asleep in the hayloft. From outside a loud voice rose
in exasperation.

'Is he in the barn again?'

Footsteps approached the entrance.

A big knotted ball of straw wiggled loose from its haystack.
With a dry scratch it left the tottering pile behind and rolled
through the barn doors and out across the yard.

'There he is! Come here, you!'

The clump of straw moved at speed. It was swiftly followed
by a dozen milkmaids. The farm reverberated with the stamp
of running feet, and the muddy yard was a tumble of gingham
skirts. An idle goose surveyed the commotion.

'Oi!'

Their caps had come unfastened and their plaited hair
tangled out behind them. The maid leading the scramble had her
arm raised, hand clenched into a fist. Some carried pitchforks.

The tumbleweed disappeared around a corner.

'Don't let him reach the paddock!'

The tumbleweed unravelled into a figure, dashing madly
through the farmyard. Roosters flapped out of his way with a
chorus of clucks. The figure leapt over a picket fence into the
alpaca pen, and the milkmaids rushed in after. The maid who

had been leading the chase pulled him up by the ear.

'Think this is funny, do you?' she said.

Puck protested uselessly; she had raised him up onto his toes.

She shook him lightly. 'You carry on startling us with all this, we'll drop our milk and curdle it,' she said. 'And there'll be worse consequences. Is that what you're after? Grain rotting in the stores and the cheese all with mould on?'

'Hadn't thought about it,' said Puck.

She let go with a snort and he landed with a splat in the mud. The alpacas, sitting in a close group at one end of the pen, serenely turned and looked at him.

'You'll stop being a menace!' The milkmaid wagged her finger, and Puck smiled back with a face dusted with flour from the biggest mill.

'Can it hurt to have some fun, miss?'

'Enough now, let me be off,' she said, leaving through the white wooden gate. 'Make yourself useful—' her breath caught as she lifted a full bucket of fresh milk in each hand, '—you can go to the kitchens and help sift flour for the sugar bread.'

Puck nodded, removing a piece of dirt from his mouth.

The milkmaids whispered between themselves as they left the pen.

'He's been sitting very still in the apple stores,' said one of them, 'pretending to be a golden delicious.'

'That must make for a sweet batch of cider,' said another. 'Let's leave him to it.' She threw a scatter of grain for the geese, who flocked around it, flapping. Soon the milkmaids' talk had turned to silence.

Puck sat there for a moment. He wiggled his toes in the soft brown mud. Then he leapt up, with a bright laugh, and sped towards the great cobblestone farmhouse.

A rusting bucket stood beside the farmhouse door filled with brackish rainwater, beside a neat row of boots for the fields. Growing up the wall was a spreading sweetpea with delicate pink flowers and a lush crop of tomatoes in red, green and gold, their rich scent carrying over the gardens. Puck breathed it in with a smile as he went inside, closing the door behind him with a heavy smack of wood.

At one end of the farm a river bubbled along, lined with upsprung bulrushes. A mill squatted along its banks, taking up helpings in a waterwheel. A weatherworn shepherd passed a maid in a ragged apron carrying a wicker basket full of pears. They stopped and bowed in greeting.

'Did you hear Puck's back?' said the shepherd.

'Aye!' The maid nodded. 'We'll be needing to watch the cows. They're getting a bit drowsy.'

The farm's pride and joy was the dairy herd — every cow had large black spots that seemed to catch the light in all sorts of colourful tints, and they produced endless bounties of thick cream until the milkers collapsed exhausted in the straw. When they weren't being milked they occupied the lushest pastures, looking out at the world from beneath their lashes. At night Puck had taken to sprinting around the cowshed, pulling faces at them.

The shepherd's expression grew serious. 'Let's keep an eye out.'

'Surely we must. I've just been to the orchard,' she added. 'All the fruit-pickers are talking about how the meadow's a mess. Tied up in one big knot. He's run off with the summer bunting again, taken it underground and looped up all the foxholes.'

67

'That's going to be trouble. Did you hear he took the plough out on his own? Let the shire horse loose and worked the entire barley field.'

'No!'

'Aye! And that's not the worst of it — he's only gone and carved a very rude drawing into the soil. You can see it ever so clear from the hill.'

The shepherd looked out towards the open fields.

'It's almost as if he's forgotten each prank as soon as he's committed it,' he said.

The maid nodded in agreement.

Inside the farmhouse at that very moment a farm worker was trudging heavily up the stairs, her face smudged with sweat and dirt from the effort of delivering new lambs. Satisfied and exhausted, she was on her way to take a bath in the old farmhouse tub. She opened the door and was blinded by a hot onrush of steam.

'Puck?' she called, her stomach sinking, knowing for sure. 'Have you had a bath?'

She fanned the steam away and saw a large space where the tub used to be. A limp sponge sat in a puddle of cooling water, next to a plug on a chain to nowhere.

'Where's the bath gone?'

By the time everyone had set out to search the farm, Puck had dragged the tub clean through the yard, leaving great ruts in the dirt, and pulled it into the biggest barn, locking the door behind him. Geese knocked on the door, banging with their beaks, but he didn't answer.

When all the farmhands finally got inside, the spacious barn was empty except for a few broken broom handles piled up in the corner. The place was quiet and the air had turned bad from an old butter churn towards the very back, left to curdle on its own.

Dinner and a Show

Bottom refilled Titania's glass from the water jug, then his own. The jug had a pendulous weight in his hand, and he wondered if it would ever run out, if it would ever become empty. He was growing light in the head.

'I'm a Changeling now?'

'That seems to be what happened. But you would've been on the brink before,' said Titania. 'It's a good thing, believe me — you're rare stuff.'

'So you collect Changelings?'

'Sort of, but no. We spend time tracing them, making sure they're best placed for their gifts. It's unusual to have one so neatly delivered to me.'

'I'd heard of them,' he said, 'but you never think it could happen to you. It's a funny old life.'

Titania lay back against the fig tree, gazing at him. 'There's a piece of orange blossom on your cheek there.'

The Loveliness sent another warm pulse through her. She took a deep breath in — and on the outskirts of Athens a great wave swelled and pushed against cliff walls, then steadily lowered itself with a fizzing new layer of white foam.

She returned to herself, and a thought occurred. 'Are you hungry?'

71

Bottom put his hands to his stomach. He couldn't remember the last time he'd eaten. 'Ravenous,' he said. 'I'd give anything for a pot of something tasty.'

Titania laughed and was treated to Bottom's broad smile. She stood and called out from the edge of the bower. 'Lilly, Blossom, Fuchsia, Butterfly — anyone who isn't busy?'

Within a moment a small group were standing among the boughs.

'How is he?' asked one of them.

Titania swept an appraising look over Bottom. 'Much better, thanks to you all,' she said. 'I'm sure you'd agree. And now it seems we're both a little hungry. Would you mind preparing something for us?'

'Of course!' The fairies spent a moment conferring in whispers about the menu, then left.

Titania knelt beside Bottom. 'Just think, most of the city is waiting for tomorrow to really let loose,' she said, raising her glass to him. 'But we're breaking the seal ahead of schedule.'

Bottom's eyes grew wide. 'What's going on tomorrow?'

Titania looked at him concerned. 'You really don't know. You've had quite a time of it.'

He nodded in agreement. 'I suppose I must have.'

'It's a state holiday for the wedding of Hippolyta and Theseus, in fact that's why I'm in town. You must've taken quite a bang to the tush for that to have slipped your mind.'

From outside the bower came shouts between the fairies, and the distant clink of cutlery. Titania could make out the flurry of movement through the fig boughs.

When she looked back at Bottom, he was transfixed by the glass of water in his hand.

72

'What is it?'

'The wedding,' said Bottom. 'I forgot. I was going.'

'*You're* going? You're shitting me!' Titania grabbed his hands and gave them a squeeze. 'A social butterfly as well! Who've you been impressing?'

He shook his head. 'Not as a guest. But it doesn't matter because I can't go now.'

Titania opened her mouth to respond. There was a gentle cough and Fuchsia ducked into the bower. She curtsied graciously towards Bottom.

'Food is ready,' she said. Her eyes flicked over his face with close attention. 'My,' she added. 'If you don't mind my saying so, you're really something.' She gave a massive wink as she shimmied back into the bush.

They stood to leave the bower and Titania linked her arm through his. 'We'll discuss it later,' she said. 'And you may as well put your dungarees back on while we're eating.'

The forest had been strung with more oil lamps. In a space between the trees the fairies had placed a small wooden table. There were two chairs made of dark oak and woven straw. The table was set with thick plates and cutlery with wooden handles, and a jug of water flavoured with apple pieces. A candle stood in a silver holder, dripping wax as the flame burned. In a glass bottle stood an arrangement of freshly-picked orchids with a spray of foliage. Bottom placed one hand on the table, balancing precariously to pull the denim trouser-leg over his large foot.

Titania pulled out a chair and gestured to Bottom to sit. He finished pulling the dungarees straps over his shoulders as he took his place opposite her.

In the centre of the table was a small bowl of olives.

Titania took one.

'They've really done a lovely job for us,' said Bottom.

'Charming of you to say so.'

'I usually warm my barley bread over yesterday's coals and take it with me to eat. There's a small hill I like to sit on upwind of the tannery.'

'Nothing quite like dining al fresco,' said Titania. 'I prefer most things outside.'

Bottom grinned and took some olives.

Buttermilk stood by the table. She was holding two plates topped with tarnished silver domes.

'We did appetizers,' she said, carefully placing Bottom's plate before him and lifting the lid.

He gazed down at his soup. It was the colour of terracotta, topped with basil leaves. Beside it were thickly-cut slices of bread, freshly baked and still warm, and some butter and salt. Bottom grabbed his spoon. 'Thank you,' he said.

Buttermilk shrugged her shoulders coquettishly before leaving.

'I said I would look after you,' said Titania.

The soup's savoury warmth soothed Bottom's insides. He looked around the forest and murmured to himself between mouthfuls. 'I can't believe I'm here and this is real,' he said. 'I feel so lucky.'

'We both do,' said Titania, looking up into the night sky. Her fingers played with a stray orchid petal, rubbing it gently into a knot.

Bottom scraped the spoon across his empty bowl. The flush of energy from the food was making his belly growl. 'Are things around here always this delicious?'

Titania looked amused. 'It's my preference,' she said. 'We try to arrange things that way.'

Bottom broke off a crust of bread and slathered it with butter.

'Let's talk about the new you,' she said approvingly, waving her fork towards him.

Bottom looked down at his dungarees. The material stretched taut over his muscular thighs.

He thought twice and then said, 'Well, my cock's bigger than it's ever been.'

At that exact moment Lilly arrived, humming happily and carrying a large plate. Bottom looked down at his feet, embarrassed, a sheepish smile spreading over his face.

Lilly wore a playful grin and nothing else. 'I'm happy to hear that about your cock,' she said. 'Here's the main course.'

She placed it in front of him. Upon the plate lay a glistening whole salmon, surrounded by fresh green leaves and pieces of lemon.

'Shall I serve you up a portion,' said Lilly, 'or would you prefer to eat direct from the platter?'

Bottom licked his lips. 'The whole thing will be fine. Thank you.' He nodded politely after her as she went.

He looked down at the plate. Then his eyes flicked to Titania for permission.

'Go ahead.'

Bottom lowered his head and ate.

Titania nibbled from her own plate and watched him. She noticed the small movements of his neck, and the way his tongue licked around his lips between bites. She felt a tender ache swell over her thoughts. She imagined wrapping her arms around as much of him as she could; pressing her feet into his firmer parts; finding any smooth private nook, dip or indent to fit herself into; inhaling the earthy smells of him. As she raised her head to the night sky and closed her eyes she let the thrum of longing move through her — and across Attica, every shrine to every god became filled with incense as bowls of perfume overflowed.

Finally Bottom raised his head. 'That was delicious,' he said. 'I mean really, wow.'

She brushed a loose strand of hair from her face. 'I hope you gave yourself some time to taste it.'

Bottom chewed slowly on a piece of watercress. 'I did,' he said, through a full mouth.

'I wish Oberon could see you,' said Titania. 'You'd like him and I'm sure he'd feel the same about you. But he's got his own evening plans tonight.'

'I'm sorry to miss him.' Bottom thought for a moment, reflecting on his evolving situation. 'I would have loved to meet Hippolyta too.'

'Everyone wants to meet Hippolyta. She's wonderful.'

'There are so many stories.' Bottom scrunched up his face in thought. 'Is it true, what I've heard, that the Amazons literally don't recognise authority?'

Titania considered it. 'Possibly,' she said.

'They also say that everyone loves them anyway, even if you're not into horses.'

'That one has a ring of truth to it,' admitted Titania.

Bottom sucked on a thin piece of lemon peel. 'And when Hippolyta marries Theseus tomorrow, will the Amazons move to Athens?'

'I heard most of the palace grounds are being remodelled to

make way for stables,' said Titania. 'So it looks like they'll be here and there.' She looked deeply into Bottom's eyes, searching there. 'Are you ready to tell me what you were supposed to be doing at the wedding?'

'Performing in a play,' said Bottom. 'But the others—'

Titania reached for her water glass. 'I understand,' she said. 'And now you think you can't go.'

'Of course I can't.' Bottom met her look.

'These acquaintances of yours,' said Titania. 'What do you think they'd make of any of us here?'

Bottom thought about it. 'I understand what you mean.'

She sipped on the water and looked at him again. For a moment he felt he could swim in her eyes.

Mustardseed and Lullaby arrived, pushing a two-tier serving trolley.

'Care to choose anything from the dessert selection?' said Lullaby.

The trolley was filled to bursting with sweet things. There were cakes marbled over with icing, decorated with spires of cream, laden with glazed fruit; shortbread biscuits with bowls of chocolate; ice creams drizzled with fruit syrup; delicate meringues piled with fresh berries. Mustardseed and Lullaby were standing proudly beside it with their fingers in the goods, tasting bits of each.

'Don't mind us,' they said.

Bottom stared in amazement. 'How do I pick here?'

Titania came to his rescue. 'Leave it with us,' she said. 'We'll serve ourselves.'

They left, taking a few more samples with them, hands and faces smeared with butter and icing. Titania rested her head in her hand and looked intensely at Bottom while he struggled with the decision. When he finally reached out a tentative hand towards a cake she leaned forwards over the table, her hair falling loosely around her face.

'Hey,' she said. Bottom's hand stopped in the air.

'I can tell you're feeling better,' said Titania. She caught his eye and trailed a hand over her neckline, directing his attention.

'Yes,' he said.

She took a small honey cake from the trolley. 'Don't let me put you off your pudding, though.'

Bottom kept his gaze steady as he watched her crumble the cake between her fingers. 'Hmmm. That's the one I wanted,' he said. He broke a shortbread finger in half, creating a small cloud of powdered sugar, and held it out towards Titania. She leaned forwards and bit it.

She chewed softly, not taking her gaze from his.

'I want you to know,' she said, 'that my king arranged this night we're having.' She brushed powdered sugar from her lips.

'He did?'

'I know, right? There's a liquid that brings on scorching lust, Bottom. I'm feeling it now. Oberon gave it to me while I was sleeping. He hopes I'll have some fun with you before dawn breaks.'

Bottom was keenly aware of the cumbersome tension stretching against the fabric of his dungarees. It felt both amazing and unrelenting. 'O,' he managed. He thought about it for a moment. 'I mean, I'd be really, really open to that, but...' He looked confused. 'Are you *sure* this was Oberon? How can you know if you were asleep?'

Titania picked up her glass and drained it. 'Bottom,' she said.

78

'Queen of the Fairies, remember? Do you think someone can put magic lube up my ass without me knowing about it?'

Bottom slowly reached out to refill their glasses, pouring from the water jug with a trembling hand, adrenalin and anticipation thumping through his veins. 'Great point.'

'Quite. The plan, if you like the sound of it, is to combine my husband's loving gift with our own natural appetites. You're really the kind I can go in for.'

'I'm glad I am. And I'm glad we've had this conversation,' he added.

Titania held out her hand. The candle flame warmed her skin as they linked fingers across the table. At his touch she shuddered — and five scattered plains across the Hellenistic world erupted as the soil involuntarily cracked open, making a wet earthy mosaic of twists and rivets that eased the parched land with glistening silt.

Lingus arrived carrying a small plate of dark chocolates. He wiped a hand theatrically across his forehead.

'Ooh, it's warm in the forest tonight,' he said. 'There's an intense charge to this table. But there is no charge to this table!' He grinned at them, then turned and left, whistling.

'You're very kind,' Titania called after him.

Bottom took a chocolate and crunched it between his teeth; the bitterness was complemented with strong peppermint. Titania put her chocolate into her mouth whole and let it soften.

'This might be difficult to hear,' she said, 'but I think you should still do the play.'

Bottom didn't answer.

'It's important to me that tomorrow goes as planned for Hippolyta and Theseus, they're very good friends of mine. So

I'm asking you, please consider it. I hope it's clear that you're under my delightful protection.'

She rose from her chair, came around and knelt beside him. She took his hand.

'Don't think about it now,' she said.

Bottom nodded. 'I'll get back to you about it.'

'Dearest,' said Titania. She kissed each of his fingers in turn. His insides flipped. Her lips were soft as her touch had been. He felt he could scale any height, reach to the top of the world.

Bottom rubbed his eyes. He looked around at the bower, noticing the play of shadows over the trees as the fairies potted about, pretending not to be looking at him.

She came around and stroked his shoulders. 'So, this dancing you do.'

Bottom smiled at the candle flame on the table. A blob of yellow wax was making its way down the shaft. 'It's only for special occasions really.'

Her hands rested softly on the back of his neck. 'You don't think this is a special occasion?'

Bottom thought about it. 'This is the most special occasion I've ever known.'

'Well then. Dance with me?'

She held out her hand to his, and he rose from the table.

They made their way between the trees, Titania beckoning Bottom to follow. A new throb from the Loveliness rose through her body as she walked. She twirled elegantly and Bottom stretched out his hands, caught her gently and pulled her in close.

Music lilted through the forest. Titania lowered her hands and squeezed her fingers around his backside.

She spoke lightly into his ear. 'Now show me how you dance on special occasions.'

The music continued to pulse through the bower, and the light from the lamps that dangled from the branches made each leaf and flower join in. Soon the fairies were jumping and cheering while Titania laughed and clapped her hands, because Bottom was slowly, gradually, and with great artistry, removing his dungarees.

Superposition

A new vibration appears, and flings across the cosmos — and at once the pearly star D. Metrius is charged. Something has been initiated. An instant ago was different, but now his nuclear core is lively: he feels distinctly squashed, he is growing denser, mashing, bucking.

He reddens at himself, his mass somehow lighter, carbonated — and he senses his feelings run upward, bracing towards his whole circumference. What has come over him? The blind heat rushes faster around his hemispheres. He giggles at himself. He wants to transmit a shout across the whole galaxy:

—   Don't you dare!

D. Metrius is the name of the White Dwarf stellar core remnant presently at 0018. His frequencies have escalated, and he is ascending through space with gravity swaying tightly behind him. His smooth surface glows so steadily it hums at his outline.

At this outermost limit of him, restless packs of photons bounce into everything they see, manufacturing collisions that respond to his presence with a flourish of hot static.

—   Oh, he gasps.

Still drowning in his own seismic sense of fullness, he cannot help an outlandish wobble as he works his way through space, free and startlingly unglued. He could get lost inside a shimmering cloud of stardust.

—   I feel larger, my limits are stretched outside themselves!

His body glows solid white under this unsurpassed and caged influence. D. Metrius is extremely aware of the atoms out there on the periphery of him, trembling with an acute sensitivity to every minor switch in the night ether. From the very tip of the spectrum he intercepts a string of signals that form into a glorious picture. His plasma flares in numerous directions: a crack in the iceberg.

Besieged with rich feeling, D. Metrius sails over a star system — its movements are languid, unwinding in a wispy display of steam. His attention is caught. He waits till he has passed into privacy and opens up to his own sense of keenness.

A fiery sparkle goes right into him and lights him up.

—   This... Is... Scandalous!

He threads through miles and miles of space, barely keeping his composure, when a new sensation makes his orbit snap into a sharper geometry.

—   Stop me! He laughs to himself.

84

He finds a gap, summoning him from the thick of huge great rocks. This belt of sharp-angled noisy shapes, fragmented and vast, are inviting D. Metrius to fly reckless. He delights in their scratch on his perimeter, a roughness that scorches their surfaces to crisp charred stardust. He knocks against the edges, yielding heat to these hung elemental blocks as he pushes through.

—　　　I'm so close!

With that, he smacks against something dense, absorbing a bumper payload of shockwaves and rotating with a lopsided kink into a temporary orbit. He spirals out. The encircling soft walls of spacetime wobble like the skin on cream, and his whole centre of gravity quivers.

As he gyrates in a mangled spin, rolling and backward, he is astounded to find his excitement remains unspent. How could this be? It's coursing through him still, expanding in the hot white iron of his metal-rich core.

He swells.
He is filled up like a perfect strawberry —

And then…

… an energetic culmination of ultraviolet is clouding the view. D. Metrius sees the two celestial bodies engaged in a frenzy of interactivity. Their shadows come apart as they sense in his approach a new astral radiation.

D. Metrius tries to conceal himself behind some dark matter.

The shadows gradually fade to become more distinct: revealing singular objects lying in pressureless space. The smudged air has the marks of Li Sander's activities and D. Metrius observes him with interest. Exhausted vapours go between them all.

Hel3na speaks:

— Don't be shy, We're all strangers here.

The encircled giantess is reclining. It could be that space itself has tilted her sideways, gradually uncovering the moon.

D. Metrius is overcome. His electrons are supercharged at the moment. He stares, goggled with wonder, dictated by his hungry attention that eats up the whole of the astral field. He can feel his energy feeding into Hel3na's, a mutual dynamo that spreads around Li Sander.

And as for the pair of twinned stars — they are spinning with iridescent vigour. Li Sander flashes D. Metrius a curt endorsement. Now this is a gesture he can get behind.

— You're a welcome sight.

— I feel welcome.

— What a night for it though!

D. Metrius spins towards the others. Their gravities tug at each other, furrowing in elaborate knots.

He brushes gently across the middle of the evening.

— So shall we make the most of it?

— That could be arranged.

— I should hope so.

— So insistent!

Li Sander's heat glides against D. Metrius's cooler atmospheres. The electrons between them spiral noiselessly into improper fractions.

— Is that expanding?

— Will you spot me?

— Go carefully.

They tower against each other in shadow — unexposed, broadcasting an eclipse.

— You're full of surprises!

— I have my secrets.

D. Metrius sends a string of waves, addressing a question to Hel3na:

—   This is ok?

Hel3na nods tightly.
Her rings have taken on a new quality of acceleration, becoming thinner than sheets.

—   Are you joining in, or what?

And over the way, the celestial body Hermia spots the party. She's a nebula. Let's bring her in.

Ass

'Oh!'

Sounds filled the air — intimate and hurried.

The figs were flicking rapidly, juddering on the boughs.

'Oh!'

The tree was receiving again and again a steady and unrelenting knock. The figs just about remained on the branches, clinging on by the funnel of their pendulous shape.

'Fuck!'

Titania's voice sang out right at the top of her register, counterpointed by low, rapid grunts and hitched breaths. The warm and wet smacking strengthened in speed as the pair jerked together at the hip in fiery bursts. Titania's eyes were wide open, staring into Bottom's face with an expression of pure hungry lust.

Beads of sweat ran between their shoulder blades and down their backs, and made breasts and chests and arms slippery and hot.

'Yes!'

At each clap of their bodies, Titania felt a ripple burn all the way through her, vibrating across her body like the tail of a struck gong.

Midnight.

She leaned her head back against the tree, her fingers holding a steady grip on Bottom's arms. She hoisted her knees higher, pressing them into either side of his body, finding deeper feeling by grinding her hips up against him.

Lullaby, Fuchsia, Blossom and the others had taken themselves away. Titania and Bottom's noises echoed naturally about the forest.

Bottom was thrusting at his full speed and power, a hot ache of pleasure burning over his thighs as he leaned his body to look down into her blissful face. He moved steadily, the small of his back held straight as his backside pumped, his cock lively against her readiness with every persistent thrust.

Bottom pulled out until the head of his erection pressed gently around Titania's moist and damp skin, then slowly moved back into her and held himself there as a tease — and Titania gasped and opened her mouth wider, staring directly into his eyes, and high in the universe new stars were born, turning on in the darkness of the galaxy like an electric light.

Titania bared her teeth and pushed herself closer onto his thighs, as if she could fuse her hips to his. Bottom began thrusting again and hot waves rolled and burst inside her, pouring over her stomach and into her teeth, making them fizz at the roots.

'Oh God!'

With one hand he stroked her face and kept his hand there, a gentle hold of her cheek and then behind to the back of her neck, spreading his fingers into her hair. His hand closed over her hair and lightly pulled, and Titania moaned and scrunched her toes. Bottom brought his head closer and they kissed, his backside still thrusting away and Titania still pushing herself out from the tree to meet him.

She kissed him with her mouth open, as if she could eat him whole. He gently ran his tongue along her lips. A deep breath shuddered through him.

Titania reached up and placed two fingers inside his mouth. He sucked on them delicately. Titania removed her fingers and gave him a coaxing look.

'You have,' whispered Bottom, between gasps, 'the most impossibly inviting behind.' He smiled happily. 'It fits in my hands and feels so...'

Titania moved her fingers down her chest, stroking over her hardened nipples and then onwards to her hips. Bottom licked his lips and raised his body slightly to give her room. Titania began gently pressing, adding pleasure from her swollen tenderness to the heady sensation rolling deep and low. At her fingers' pressure she closed her eyes and leaned her head back against the tree, her mouth opening in a silent cry.

Bottom's gaze travelled eagerly, trying to look at all of her at once: he sunk from her eyes to the weight of her breasts, the nip of her waist, the slope of her belly. His chest was rising and falling with heavy breaths.

They continued, and rows of leaves rustled in waves with each thrust. Titania opened her mouth in a great stretch of silent joy. Bottom moaned out loud, a bellowing bestial cry: he closed his eyes and his world was filled with the smell of Titania, the slick feeling of her wetness, and the utterly welcome demands her body was making of his.

*

A rummaging, a clink of bottles. Then, a satisfied roar.

'*There* you are! I found it, Oberon. Right at the back of the cabinet!'

Between the pillars strode a muscular figure wearing a black toga edged with gold. A laurel wreath sat upon his noble head, the leaves shining against the dark curls of his hair. In one hand he held a crystal decanter filled with rich golden liquid.

'This is one of the finest whiskies you'll ever taste, my friend!' cried Theseus, founder and high ruler, Duke of Athens.

He held the bottle aloft.

'You're true to your word, I hope,' said Oberon. 'No fobbing me off with the cheap stuff.'

'I only associate with quality. Come here you.' And Theseus pulled Oberon into a tight embrace, slapping him roughly on the back. Then he held Oberon by the shoulders, and the two of them stood there in the centre of the room, beaming at each other.

'You're looking good,' said Theseus.

Oberon was wearing a long jacket of deepest midnight blue, and a full set of antlers for the occasion. The antlers stood proudly either side of his head, forking into several sharp ends, glistening a stately shade of golden brown.

'Many thanks,' said Oberon. 'I awoke like this!'

Theseus and Oberon perched themselves upon two high stools at one end of the club, where their dignified faces were reflected in the polished wood of the bar. Theseus poured the liquor into two fine whisky tumblers.

'Well then. Here's to the future.' Theseus raised his glass, affecting a serious air.

'I don't really experience it in those terms but let's go with it,' said Oberon. 'Cheers.'

Their glasses clinked and the club became silent for a moment as they entered a period of steady, thoughtful sipping.

'So tonight marks the end of your lonely governance and tomorrow a new era of shared collaboration,' remarked Oberon.

'Can't come soon enough, my old boy. She said she's going to teach me to negotiate the Amazonian way.'

'I've heard it's effective,' said Oberon.

They were in a discrete and private villa in one of the more reputable districts of Athens. In the air hung the gentle aftertang of fine cigar smoke. Marble busts of former members of the club looked proudly over the decor with stone eyes. Great scrolls of philosophy, poetry and geometry filled shelves across the walls, all display copies, gilt at the edges.

'What I'm really excited about is the revelling,' said Theseus. 'I do enjoy a state holiday!' He sighed with satisfaction. 'It's so good to see you.'

Oberon nodded sagely. 'How long has it been?'

'Long enough for Athens to turn upside-down.' Theseus grinned meaningfully.

'What, hosting the Amazons? You like horses though,' said Oberon. He put his empty glass back down on the bar. 'Even if they do make a massive mess.'

'That's not quite what I meant. But tonight I'm feeling wonderfully calm. Everything's ready, no more delegating to do.'

'You can sit back and enjoy it.'

'Oh I intend to. The entertainment I think will be… historic.'

'Have you been plotting again, Theseus?'

His eyes twinkled. 'This wedding is a political world event. I'm using this platform to represent our national story in a way that does service to its ideals. We're going to explain Athens to the world, and to itself.'

'Sounds noble,' said Oberon. 'What's the plan?'

'We've commissioned some city artisans to develop a show — that's the big idea, who's doing it — people from all sorts of local trades, not just the acting trade. This method will celebrate our Democratic system... and they'll be authentic in the moment.' Theseus beamed, spreading his arms triumphantly.

Oberon glugged more whisky from the decanter. He peered down at his glass, considering it. It was full. He carefully added another small splash.

'You're always pushing boundaries,' he said.

Theseus looked pleased.

Oberon leaned over the bar, his antlers suggesting for a brief moment that he might be about to charge, and brought out another bottle for them both. 'This reminds me of the good old days,' he said. 'Me and you.'

Theseus made to draw from an imaginary dagger. 'You take that back, villain! It's *still* the good old days!'

Oberon raised his hands in mock surrender, then picked up his glass and downed the contents. 'Do you remember,' he said, 'when you lifted that massive boulder—'

Theseus bent his head and leaned it against Oberon's shoulder. 'Oh no,' he said, his voice suddenly low with embarrassment. 'Don't.'

Oberon ruffled Theseus's head affectionately, dislodging further the dignified laurel wreath. 'You picked it *right* up — just because they said you wouldn't be able to. You did that enigmatic smile of yours, ripped your smock off and *boom*. Boulder in the air.'

'I was a bit of a show-off back then,' muttered Theseus.

Strung across the Amazon crown was a pair of lacy underpants.

'On and forward!' cried Hippolyta, raising her sword in the air.

The crowd of Amazons cheered and the party galloped on, bellowing their favourite war cries over the clatter of thunderous hooves.

The party galloped through the narrow streets of Athens. Window-shutters opened in the villas and people leaned out to cheer them along — greeting them with a chorus of screams and wild shouts, waving homemade banners. In return, Amazons flipped rude gestures and spurred their horses faster, cackling into the balmy night.

And Hippolyta rode at the front of the cavalry, surrounded by a cloud of dust kicked up by her stallion: standing in the stirrups, holding the reins in one hand, baring muscular legs beneath her skirt of leather.

Hippolyta led the Amazons through an alleyway and out into a civic square bursting with townsfolk, who erupted into giddy cheers at the sight of them. An Amazon wearing thigh-high sandals began spinning her slingshot — to *ooohs* and *aaahs* from the crowd she lengthened the rope until it reached full acceleration, twirling at dizzying speed above her head. The crowd parted as the Amazons galloped their horses on a victory lap around the perimeter.

Two great Amazon warriors pulled up level with Hippolyta, still moving at full speed. The first — who was one of the brides-maids — held her bow in one hand, steering the horse with the other. She leaned towards her queen, shouting over the noise.

'The pomegranate vendor says, there's a bath house with a steam-room that goes all night, two streets over,' she cried, gesturing in the direction.

'Add it to the longlist!' shouted Hippolyta, pulling on the reins and leaning her weight to take a corner. The horse snorted and tossed its head as people jumped out of the way.

'See that pink vase on the plinth?' yelled the second Amazon, who was Hippolyta's Maid of Honour. 'Up on that balcony? Reckon I can hit it? Watch this.'

Hippolyta nodded once.

The crowd were doing a Mexican wave that rippled along with the riders. The Maid of Honour raised herself until she stood on the stirrups. She took an arrow from the quiver at her back, pulled it across the bow, held it a moment to build the tension, then let go. All eyes followed the arrow as it sailed from one side of the square to the other.

In the distance a solitary voice cried: '*My vase!*'

There came the sound of shattering pottery. The square exploded with cheering. The Maid of Honour sat back down onto her galloping steed, making one hand into a fist.

'*Yesssss,*' she said.

The bridesmaid Amazon pulled a small bottle from her satchel, removed the cork, necked some of the booze and threw it over to Hippolyta, who caught it in one hand and drained it.

'Let's get out of this square,' Hippolyta said, wiping her mouth with the back of her arm. She raised herself on the stirrups and turned to address the horde who followed her.

'Right, we're fucking off somewhere else!' she said.

They cheered in answer, raising weapons and fists, and the unruly cavalry thundered on. The Amazon with a shaved head casually lopped an ear off one of the more saccharine statues as she passed it.

'What now?' cried the Amazon who had an L-Plate dangling over her back. 'Shall we head up to the Parthenon, find somewhere to go dancing on the way?'

'What about that bath house?' said the Amazon in thigh-high sandals. 'Let's all try and fit in the sauna.'

They continued on, pounding through the dusty side streets to rapturous applause.

The Amazon in silver armour had an idea. 'Let's go to the university and moon the scholars!'

'Agreed!' cried Hippolyta. The horses whinnied as they took a sharp side-turn.

'We'll have to get past security,' added the Maid of Honour, as everyone splashed through an ornamental fountain.

And they galloped up to a high point in the city where they swung from their horses, high-fiving and banging their bodies together with a loud cymbal-crash of colliding breastplates. As the Athenian military guard laughed along, the Amazons flipped their pleated leather skirts up and wiggled their bums over the parapet.

*

Titania weaved her fingers into Bottom's fur and breathed in the sweet musk of his scent, noticing the tension of the muscles in his legs. She was kneeling before him.

Leaves brushed over the back of his neck. He stroked her shoulders with his thumb, pressing gently in a caressing squeeze.

Titania gripped her hand gently between his legs, around

the weight of skin that hung there, and she pulled on it slightly as she moved her head down over his length.

She ran her tongue over every ridge and smooth edge, rubbing the tip against the roof of her mouth where it fit smoothly; she wanted to fill herself up with the salty heat of him. She raised and lowered, running her lips and tongue over the smooth skin, dipping her head with a strength of movement that made Bottom gasp, over and over.

She sucked slowly as she pulled him out. He stroked her hair. Titania tipped her head back to look at him, her mouth wet and dripping.

Bottom raised her gently and wrapped his arms around her, and holding across the small of her back lifted her clean from the floor. She folded her legs around him, clinging to his shoulders, pressing her face into the side of his neck and laughing quietly with delight. He carried her across the bower and laid her down on a pillow of soft moss.

'Let me give you something,' he said.

Her back arched as he kissed her face and down her neck, moving lower, kissing over her breasts and across her stomach. He followed kisses with licks, skimming his hands across her body. Titania wiggled as Bottom trailed his fingers down her hips and lightly over the flossy hair below.

Slowly his hands moved down to the softness between her thighs. He looked up at her, his face poised. She smiled at him and nodded happily.

His lips slowly pressed down upon the gentle folds, running along the warm flower of her sex, and his tongue traced over the skin, moving steadily. She shuddered as he applied pressure, lapping her up.

Titania lay back, arms thrown above her head. Beyond the ripe figs the universe began blinking. She looked down to Bottom's head slowly moving between her legs. She lowered a hand to grip his hair. His tongue found a pressure point in the centre of her cunt, and her mouth opened in surprise.

'Oh—'

He ran his tongue around, flicking and teasing. Titania let her head drift back onto the moss and the surface of a distant blood moon became molten with sudden onrushes of lava. Bottom moved his tongue quickly up and down and up again. His hands held firmly onto her hips. She bucked her hips against the pressure, pushing against him then back into the soft dirt.

Bottom moved lower.

He hoisted her higher and dipped his head to kiss her ring, and ran a finger across it. Then he moved in with his tongue.

Titania let out one long outward breath. A meteor shower sailed through the black sky, thousands of burning comets leaving vivid gold trails.

She turned onto her side, baring herself to him there. He began kissing between her mound and her asshole, running his tongue over and inside the warm pinkness.

The Loveliness that glazed Titania's bottom finally touched his tongue. A deep rush of heat raced through from his lips to the end of his tail.

He knelt up and swallowed, his throat fizzing and his tongue sensitive and heated with the strange energy of the liquid.

'I've got so many ideas,' he said. 'We're not going to run out of time are we?'

Titania sat up.

'No.'

She wrapped her arms around Bottom and they kissed, their mouths open and greedy for each other, and Titaina felt warm pearls of Loveliness between their tongues. She stroked her hands down his back, and looking into his eyes, placed her finger in her own mouth. Then she lowered her hand again, spreading his bottom cheeks and slipping one finger inside.

A deep moan went through him, steadily. Titania smiled and kept her gaze on him, and her finger gently teased the inside of Bottom's hole, going slowly deeper. The soft ridge of his body pulsed around her finger.

Bottom's eyes were wide open and his breath came in hurried gasps. Titania felt a rumble through the woods and faint vibrations as a far-away star went supernova.

*

'Just say if I'm moving through these too quickly,' said Theseus, uncorking a bottle with a dagger. 'Now, this is a particularly good single malt. It was a peace offering from Sparta.'

Oberon eyed the bottle as if it were a deadly snake. 'And the same to you,' he said warily. His voice had grown a little thick. 'Let me know when you need to slow down.'

They maintained eye contact with each other as they took a long slow sip. Then Oberon put both hands on the bar and lowered his head so Theseus wouldn't see his face contort.

'Are all your political meetings this jolly?' he said, when he got his breath back.

'They can be. Diplomacy requires its fair share of social lubrication.' Oberon's eyes briefly went wide. Theseus looked at him. 'What are you smirking at?'

'I was just thinking about Titania,' said Oberon.

'I see.' Theseus did a leer and pulled a face, wiggling his fingers over his noble aquiline nose. It looked vaguely obscene, though his exact meaning was ambiguous.

'Whatever it is you're thinking — and I'll admit I have no idea — it's not that,' said Oberon. 'We had a heated discussion earlier. Ended up falling out a bit.' He flicked his eyes to Theseus to make his announcement. 'And I've done an apology gesture. It's a very nice idea, my apology gesture,' he added, and he grinned as he reached for the bottle. 'Anyway that's what I was thinking about.'

'Sounds like you're not too obstinate to ask forgiveness where you ought,' said Theseus. He lightly bounced his finger on the end of Oberon's nose. 'Well done.'

Oberon finished the whisky and put the glass back onto the bar upside-down. Theseus put his hand on his own forehead in disbelief.

'I told you not to down it,' he said, as Oberon sat there juddering on the bar stool. 'It's mainly supposed to be about tasting and you know how you get.'

'You're only saying that because it's expensive.'

'It's not expensive. It's priceless. Look, about the thing with your good lady Titania: a gesture of apology is still only that. Make sure she hears it from you personally also.'

Oberon's smile grew thoughtful, even as his lips were still chewing on the aftertaste of the whisky. 'Your world-famous reputation for wisdom is well deserved,' he said.

Theseus's face became maudlin. 'You say that,' he said, and he looked towards the ceiling in a tragic attitude, 'but you know the story behind what happened with the Minotaur.'

101

Oberon nodded sagely and reached for the small ash-tray of peanuts in the centre of the bar. He'd heard the Minotaur story before.

'My finest achievement,' said Theseus.

'Except for the boulder,' said Oberon. 'And there's your other achievements. Hey. Let's do your ten greatest achievements!'

Theseus shook his head. 'Not now,' he said. 'My point is, I might never have defeated the Minotaur without taking council from Ariadne. I've got this reputation for wisdom but my finest trick wasn't even my idea. I'm the one who did the slaying, but it wasn't me who came up with the string — I would have been royally fucked down there.'

Theseus slowly lowered his head until his forehead rested completely on the bar. His voice mumbled up from the polished wood: 'The woman always gives you the string.'

'What are you talking about?' Oberon grabbed another fistful of peanuts. 'It was still you who went into the labyrinth. Just give her proper credit for the string.'

Theseus's head remained flat on the bar. 'Yes you're right. It's embarrassing. She should be on the pots.'

Oberon considered the problem. 'So make some more,' he said gleefully, putting his hand to his mouth and filling his face with peanuts.

*

Markos liked working as a blacksmith. He'd been one all his life. It was challenging and it was satisfying, he got to meet people, and he could take pride in creating things that were well-crafted, beautiful and useful (he generally aimed for two out of those three). He pushed his bellows together until the coals glowed red then took up his hammer, watching the metal become a vivid orange block in the heat. He had allowed his apprentice to retire early — she'd asked for the evening off to help with preparations for the local wedding festivities — but Markos himself was behind on a bulk order of axe-heads that had come in at the last minute, and was working late into the night. Above the door of the workshop was a pair of tongs crossed above a horseshoe, the symbols of that particularly steamy god of blacksmiths and fireworkers, Hephaestus.

Markos flattened the axe-head against the anvil, turning the handle with a master's sense of balance, knocking the edge into paper-thin sharpness. Regular heavy clangs were singing out through the workshop. Finally he held the metal tong aloft and admired the shape of the blade. One down. He plunged the finished axe-head into the water and the shop filled with pale steam. The loud hissing masked the sound of hooves approaching. This meant Markos was having a restful moment before returning to the hammer, wiping his face with a cloth, when the door burst open and an athletic woman in armour of leather and bronze entered, followed immediately by a dozen more.

'*WEAPONS!*' cried the Maid of Honour, striding into the shop and looking about, her hands on her hips.

Markos quickly edged himself behind the counter.

More Amazons squeezed into the shop, nodding approvingly at the rows of blades and sickles mounted on the walls. They unhooked display items and tested their weight, making a few trial swishes with their arms, and clustered together, talking excitedly.

The Maid of Honour headed immediately towards Markos.

After a moment fiddling about in her breastplate she brought out a crumpled piece of parchment. She placed it on the counter.

'Commission for you,' she said. Her breath smelled of wine. Markos tried not to lean backwards too obviously. 'I want you to make this for me. Can you do it tonight? I pay well.'

Markos looked down at the scribble. 'I do make blades,' he ventured.

The Amazon stabbed a finger onto the parchment excitedly. 'Look at this bit!'

Markos peered at the drawing again.

'What I want,' the Amazon explained, 'is a sword where the handle is *also* a blade. So it's basically twice the sword everyone else has.'

'*Attack!*' cried the Amazon in silver armour, holding a sword out at full stretch. Her opponent, the Amazon with the L-Plate, quickly unhooked a sword from the wall display and lunged forward to meet her. The other Amazons formed a circle around them. The dramatic *clang* of high-stakes hand-to-hand combat filled the workshop.

'Please!' cried Markos. 'Not in here!'

The Amazon in silver armour nodded at Markos with an expert's approval. 'They've got a fine balance,' she said. 'You make good swords.'

In spite of the helplessness he was feeling, a swell of pride increased the net weight of Markos's soul.

Then something new caught the Amazon in silver armour's eye. She buckled the sword from the wall display to her waist. 'Ooh, look how many of *these* there are!' she said.

The Amazons clustered around the buckets of arrowheads, letting them fall through their fingers like grains of corn in a flour mill. Markos caught the high jingle of them being loaded into pockets and satchels.

'Hippolyta will ensure that you are paid,' said the Amazon with thigh-high sandals, turning to face Markos with hands full of arrowheads. 'We don't carry local currency.'

'She's just getting some food,' added the Amazon in silver armour.

Markos was growing fraught. His attention was being pulled in all directions. Amazons were running around the place. He wanted to keep an eye on his stock, make sure the fighting didn't damage anything, stop people touching things they ought not to. He glanced at his work in progress and noticed the fire had grown out of control and molten metal was bubbling over the sides.

The Maid of Honour cleared her throat impatiently. 'Hey.'

Slowly, the warrior leaned further over the counter, eyeballing Markos with glittering fury. 'Master craftsperson,' she said. 'Are you going to make me this sword that's made out of sword or not?'

*

The bar was filled with decanters. A bottle lay on its side, gently rolling back and forth. From its neck a dribble of golden liquid pooled slowly over the polished wood. In the puddle was a wobbly reflection of Theseus's sombre face.

'You know what people ask me?' he said, making patterns in the whisky with his fingers. 'Or at least I see them thinking it. Hoity-toity people who reckon they know best. They think we're incompatible, Hippolyta and I. I know why as well: it's about the horses. And I'm like: no, it's about communication. I told Hippolyta she can put in as many stables as she likes, just leave me my hedge maze. And that's compromise.'

Oberon nodded. He was taking in approximately every third word. 'Eighty pointy people?'

Theseus frowned. 'What?'

Oberon realised he didn't quite know. He looked around for a clue.

Theseus rubbed his face and pushed a lock of hair out of his eyes, knocking the laurel wreath into a rakish angle. 'Obviously.' He looked Oberon over. 'You all right?'

Oberon was clutching tightly to the bar. The whole club was pitching dramatically left and right. 'The thing is...' said Oberon.

Theseus looked at Oberon with an expression that told him distinctly the night was nowhere near over.

Oberon adapted. 'I'm completely fine.'

Theseus stood and leaned over the bar, picking up a new and heavy item from behind it.

Oberon followed his movement with a worried air. 'What's this now?'

'Ouzo,' said Theseus, uncorking the bottle of cloudy liquid. 'Naturally.'

Oberon sighed deeply, like he just realised he'd been treading dog poo around his own house.

Two more glasses were filled to the brim, then raised and clinked together.

Oberon went first. He put the empty shot glass on the bar upside-down, his eyes screwed closed.

Theseus gulped the liquid down, and grimaced. 'Sometimes

I worry our time is passing and our best days are behind us,' he said, all at once.

Oberon's mouth made the shape of his initial.

'Honestly.' Theseus's hand was curled around his glass, rotating it slowly. 'When I think about the good old days—'

'Like with that boulder! Can you remember, you picked it up.'

'All the way up. But now—'

'You threw it into the woods! You weren't even in the woods yourself at the time. What trajectory!' Oberon shook his head in wonder. His antlers knocked against a lighting fixture and the room dipped in and out of darkness. 'You've got so many heroic stories,' he said. He frowned and scratched his head at the base of his antlers, becoming serious. 'Although you do know it's actually a terrible idea to throw things into the woods.'

'I was young then. But that's my point. You only have to look around the nearest fresco — take that one, there.' Theseus gestured around with his glass, spilling drops of liquor over the bar top. He leaned his head to the side to peer at the mural, which covered the entire wall. 'Okay so, that's not a very good example because I am actually on that one. But I'm telling you, there are new heroes all the time, sometimes I wonder how I'm supposed to stay relevant.'

Oberon squinted into the gloom. 'That fresco seems a bit smudged from here,' he said. 'I can't tell if you're defeating the Minotaur or feeding a cat.'

Theseus double checked. 'Minotaur,' he said. 'You can tell by my sandals.'

'And you wore that loincloth?'

'Something similar,' said Theseus, wrinkling his nose.

'They were all the rage.'

'Each to their own,' said Oberon. 'Theseus, why are we looking at the wall?'

Theseus pushed the laurel wreath out of his eyes. 'I'm just saying there are so many hotshot legends these days,' he said. 'The bar's higher.'

'Is it?!' Oberon looked around in panic from his tall stool. His antlers pinged against the drop-crystals of the chandelier, making a tinkling sound.

'No what I'm saying is, it's not enough to throw a boulder into a forest anymore. You've got to keep ringing the changes.'

Oberon's face pulled together in thought. He placed a friendly hand on Theseus's thigh and gave a supportive squeeze. 'If it's not enough anymore, that's *because* you did it.'

Theseus jabbed Oberon in the breastbone with a finger that wore a heavy signet ring inscribed with the sacred crest of Athens. 'I'm not a big speech kind of person,' he said. 'But I would like to say: *you*, Oberon. You are the guy. You know? You're the guy.'

Oberon put his arm around Theseus. 'We're *both* the guy!'

They held on tightly and shook each other.

*

Titania and Bottom were a sweaty heap, fucking in the soil. She lay on her back with her legs over his shoulders, baring her teeth at him.

His cock was deep in her bottom. Her eyes flashed as he slipped in and out.

Bottom bent his head to lap his tongue over her mouth, and she caught his tongue and bit it gently. She grinned up at him triumphantly, holding his tongue between her teeth. A sheen of sweat glowed across her forehead and shoulders. She released his tongue and let him kiss the side of her neck.

Titania felt a new pressure rising somewhere deep and knew she was going to come.

Bottom felt the change. His breath was deep and powerful through his chest. He gazed into her eyes intensely.

Her hair was sticking to her shoulders with sweat. Her round cheeks pressed into the soil and bounced in time to his pushes. She put her hands either side of his face and looked into him.

Then, the beginnings of a build: down in the base of her, slowly filling with warmth and all the force of a crashing wave bursting with pale sea-foam.

Bottom kept pushing, low and steady.

Titania lowered a hand onto herself, rubbing over her moist tenderness.

With her fingers cupped inside, she could feel her own heat, as well as the movement of Bottom's thrusts and her cunt being tightly pressed at both sides.

She leaned her back further into the soil, pushing her shoulder blades into the warm dry dirt.

The build deep down continued to boil upwards, a growing rhythm quickening beyond his pushes, rippling and unstoppable like the waves of the tide coming in. All the way in, and over. She emptied herself in his eyes, fastening her grip on his tense upper-arms that filled her hands with tight wide muscle, stretching upwards and through to his chest.

And —

She opened her body and let the wave crash down and through her with the force of the sea, waves of white horses tossing their manes, a steady hotness that spread everywhere, that rushed over her and burst through from the top, right down to her depths, that whipped her about in a row of rapid jolts that completed as her mouth opened into a round, sticky O.

The force of her orgasm made Titania rub harder onto Bottom, and her eyes flicked closed as pleasure rolled over her body and overpowered it with pops of joy like bubbles bursting over her nipples and stomach.

Stars locked into sparkling new constellations in the sky, burning their new shape into the night.

Titania breathed out. They slowed down, still pulsing together. Titania leaned her head into Bottom's muscled arms.

Bottom's thighs and stomach began to quake.

'Let me, here,' said Titania. She straightened her legs off his shoulders and positioned herself behind him. She took hold of his flushed erection, moving her hand back and forth along its length, her breasts pressed into his back and her head forwards against his cheek. Feeling him grow more still and strong, vibrations from her hand spread through him, and then Bottom's eyes became glassy and a jet of shining white mess sprayed enthusiastically out in joyous release and spilled over the bower, shooting upwards in a clear arc and landing in a string over the leaves and the mosses. The taller grasses were bent over at the stems, weighed down with thick daubs of salty dew.

Titania stroked with her fingers more gently as she took him through it. His breath was coming in deep gulps, expanding his chest. He continued to spatter forth between small pauses, dashing out in juts.

An ongoing trickle from him ran down over Titania's fingers. She pressed her face into him happily.

*

Spicy chilli tomato dribbled down Hippolyta's chin.

'This sauce,' she said, her words muffled through the food. 'How come I've never had one of these before?'

She turned her head to the side to fit more in, pushing the bread into her mouth with both hands. She looked about for more wine to wash it down with.

The Maid of Honour pointed to Hippolyta. 'So the one she's got, that's the most typical Athenian one?' she asked. She was standing on tiptoes to address the woman in the apron who operated the wagon. The woman nodded and flipped another round of pitta breads over the sizzling hotplates.

'Okay, I'll have one of those,' said the Maid of Honour. 'I want to eat what you all eat!'

There were cheers from the gathered crowd of fans, who had clustered in the alleyway. Some of the Amazons were signing their togas.

The Amazon in thigh-high sandals stuck her head through the wagon window. 'Can we get loads more as well,' she added. 'To take away.'

'I'm going to make it illegal not to eat these,' said Hippolyta. A piece of lettuce landed wetly on the stone steps. She pointed at the wagon owner. 'You may display the royal crest on your vehicle from now on, by the way.' She tapped her crown, smearing sauce over it.

Amazons were giving earnest hugs to random people in the crowd. The Amazon in silver armour was explaining the slider mechanism on her crossbow to an eager group of children.

'... get 'em right in the lungs,' she said.

Hippolyta rested her head on the cool stone of the wall. 'I can hear the sea,' she whispered.

More Amazons were standing in an eager queue in front of the wagon. The Amazon at the front of the queue raised her hand. 'Ooh! Did you remember I want double sauce?'

The wagon vendor picked up the bottle and gently shook it.

Hippolyta crumpled the paper into a ball and let it drop to the floor. 'That was epic.' She closed her eyes for a moment, savouring the aftertaste. Then she stood and, picking up the wrapper, crossed over and carefully placed it in the wooden bucket beside the wagon. 'Keep Athens tidy,' she said.

'After kebabs,' suggested the Amazon with an unusual piercing, 'who fancies a swim?'

Hippolyta looked deadly serious. 'I'm up for that,' she said.

They all had a pitta now, and the scent of rich spices and roasted meat filled the air. They took great bites and grunted in approval as they munched. Tomato juice splattered onto their sandals.

'Tell you what,' said Hippolyta. 'Let's go in the sea but stay on the horses. They'll be fine right up to the flanks. And let's go properly bareback.' She wiped her sticky hands on the back of her pleated leather skirt, then began undoing the clasp. 'Will you look after our armour until we get back?' she addressed the wagon owner as her skirt slid off. The woman nodded, still chopping onions.

There were cheers from the crowd as the Amazons began

unbuckling their armour and unfastening straps. Weapons and breastplates clattered to the ground.

Wearing only her helmet, Hippolyta swung herself up onto her stallion. She clutched the mane with one hand and raised her other into the air.

'*Here comes the fucking bride!*'

Her horse reared on his hind legs and galloped towards the moonlit beach. Kicking up sand, Hippolyta was followed by a host of roaring naked Amazons into the shining blackness of the water.

RETURN OF THE KING

It was not yet officially the morning after, although midnight had long passed, and Oberon was staggering through the wood in a more-or-less straight line. As he went he mumbled a song for which Theseus had taught him the harmony parts.

Occasionally he swerved beneath the weight of his great antlers. When he did this with particular speed, surprising even himself, low hanging branches rattled along his head like marimbas.

'Inconvenient!' objected Oberon whenever this happened, fumbling around in the dark to find his balance.

But he knew the route, and it wasn't too long before he emerged into the clearing with its slumbering fairies. He looked about, running a hand through his hair. The fig tree stood proudly on.

Oberon walked towards the bower, the forked antlers shrinking into his usual horns. When he reached the fig tree he parted the boughs and peered in. Through the darkness he could make out the shape of Titania and Bottom lying entwined together on the ground.

'Hey it worked!'

He beamed and pushed his way through towards them, taking off his shoes and socks.

He could make out the gentle glow of Titania's bare skin, and as his eyes adjusted he saw the contentment in her face. He admired the soft strength of Bottom's chest and arms. A thin blanket lay loosely over them.

Oberon's eyes grew happy with tears. 'You look so comfy.'

He gently removed the rest of his clothes and knelt down slowly, feeling out for the steadiness of the ground. Then he crawled towards Bottom and Titania, carefully and with great attention, as if looking for something precious dropped in the dust. He took hold of one corner of the soft blanket and got in with them. He wrapped his arms around Titania, and she snuggled into his embrace. Her own arms were resting gently over Bottom's body, who lay there smiling in his sleep. Oberon closed his eyes. Then he raised his head slightly and squinted at the fig branches, not terribly reassured that they weren't spinning.

'Better hold on anyway,' he said to himself, resting his head flat again. He clutched tightly to the edges of the blanket until sleep rose up to meet him.

The three of them dozed there like that until the wood became pale and ghostly with pre-dawn light.

The break of day lifted the stillness of the bower. Titania put her hands to her face and rubbed her eyes. A new flower had grown in the patch where Bottom's cum had landed, a spray of iridescent snowdrops with fine petals.

Beside her came a low, anguished groan.

'He's back!' she said, smiling upwards to the top-most branches of the fig tree.

Oberon curled up in a ball like a puppy, his head tucked under his arm.

Titania stroked his hair. 'Have fun last night?' she asked, sympathetically.

Oberon uncurled himself a little, though he kept his face covered. 'I've got a slamming headache,' he said through his fingers. 'Theseus fed me four-hundred-year-old whisky shots. How are you?'

'Can't lie, great actually.'

Titania sat up and rested herself against a prominent tree root with the blanket over her thighs. Oberon remained curled up against Titania's side, his hand resting lightly over her legs. Titania glanced over at Bottom, who was snoring gently.

'I'm so sorry about yesterday,' said Oberon, his voice muffled against her.

Titania felt the smooth crook of his horns press lightly into her body. She stroked his hair with one hand. 'Yesterday was a lot,' she said.

Oberon sat up — the kohl under his eyes was smudged all over and his hair was plastered to his face — and tenderly took her hand. 'I mean it,' he said.

The straight line of delicate snowdrops that had sprung up around Bottom's cumshot were opening their petals in the warmth of the sun, bobbing their shiny heads on the stems.

'I've decided I forgive you,' said Titania.

Oberon held her look. 'Oh thank goodness for that,' he said.

Then he added: 'Excuse me my love, but I can't remain upright a moment longer.' He sank back onto the ground. 'My head feels like a dry old sponge.'

Bottom turned over on his side and continued to snore. Titania placed one hand on his shoulder, still stroking Oberon's hair with the other. There was a chorus of *good mornings* from outside the bower and Fuchsia, Lingus and Lilly pushed the fig leaves aside and came through. Titania mouthed *good morning* at them, beaming, a guy in each hand.

'Can we bring you anything?' they said.

'Only more water for now, thank you,' said Titania.

Oberon opened one eye and frowned. 'Titania. Where did the Changeling go?'

'He left early for a run,' she said. 'He's carrying a marble statue as well, to make it more difficult.'

'We knew he was good,' said Oberon.

There was a polite cough and Blossom stood by the bower.

'Good morning,' said Blossom. 'You look very well rested.'

'*She* does,' muttered Oberon.

Titania frowned. 'Is everything all right?'

Blossom's polite smile had a hint of nervousness to it. She held herself straight and anxious.

'Um,' she said. 'We wondered if either of you might know anything about Puck.'

Titania's arms were draped across Oberon's shoulders. 'What about Puck?'

'We can't find him.'

'What?'

'None of us can find him. I'm a bit worried.'

Titania moved her hand down onto Oberon's back. She chewed on her lip, thinking.

'I don't think he's in trouble,' said Blossom quickly. 'I think he's hiding.'

'What's this now?' said Oberon. 'What happened?'

'Puck had a difficult night.' She stroked Bottom's cheek. 'Our new friend had quite a hostile reception.'

Oberon nodded once. He looked down at the ground.

Dawn light spread through the forest lifting the dusky blue and greys.

'Thank you Blossom,' said Titania. 'Don't fret about Puck.' She looked at Oberon. 'I'll go and find him.'

Oberon put his hands up to his head. His pounding headache was back; he sat with the new details of the night's events. 'Oh fuck,' he concluded.

Titania closed her eyes and opened them again.

'I know where he is,' she said.

Oberon held Titania's face gently and ran his thumb across her brow. Then he removed his hands in surprise. '*There?*'

Titania shrugged.

'He did have a holiday booked in,' said Oberon. 'Odd choice.'

'He'll have his reasons. And I've always fancied visiting.' She looked up and addressed Blossom. 'Please let the others know that I'm on it.'

Blossom looked lighter. 'Thank you,' she said, and she exited the bower.

Titania prepared to stand, and Oberon placed his hands lightly on her arms and addressed her.

'Puck and I planned this,' he said. 'I should make amends, why don't you stay here with your new lover?'

'Oberon, you're about as hungover as I've ever seen you,' said Titania looking at his suffering face. 'Give me some time. I'll try to get Puck along to the wedding.'

Titania stood naked in the centre of the bower. She stretched her arms towards the sky and dawn light spread over her body. She looked down at the King of the Fairies, curled up in the blanket.

'My Oberon,' she said.

'Hurry back,' said Oberon, a little too loud. He screwed up his face at a fresh twang of pain in his head.

'Rest up, you two,' said Titania. 'I won't be long.' She gestured towards Bottom. 'Make sure this one gets a nice breakfast.'

Oberon lay down again next to Bottom. Bottom turned over in his sleep and wrapped his arms around Oberon, and the two of them lay there together as Titania stepped out of the bower and vanished.

Tube Stop

'Anyway, turned out it was a bug on my app.'

From unseen tunnels came the loud metal screaming of trains pulling heavily in and groaning their way out. Among the most densely cramped part of the crowd two figures arrived onto the platform.

'God, do I need another coffee? I don't even remember buying this.' The man had a free newspaper under his arm and a leather satchel slung over his shoulder. He glanced at his associate with admiration. 'Must say you're looking very elegant, Tanya. What field do you work in?'

She wore a tailored white trouser suit with a slim jacket buttoned once at the waist, and her face was mostly hidden by a pair of oversized tinted sunglasses. The commuters surrounding her stole second, third, fourth glances. Everyone on the platform was tightly packed together, yet Titania stood in a spotlight of calm.

Silently she took the coffee from him, had a single sip and gave it back.

'Special effects,' she said. 'There you are,' she added, as two orange lamps became visible at the far end of the tunnel.

'I knew you were a creative,' the man said. He raised his voice to a shout as the train pulled into Bank with a screaming dying hiss: 'Was thinking media or fitness or something!'

The crowd bunched itself further into clumps in front of the doors.

'Let me get your email,' he said desperately, 'I'll pass on the info I mentioned about *Last Minute Tickets*.'

'Won't be a moment,' murmured Titania, swerving neatly as everyone pushed forwards. Smoothly navigating the crowd she walked to the far end of the platform, where the train ended in big windows opaque with dirt. She dipped her sunglasses down to cast an eye over the platform, then with a single movement took hold of the large metal handle, swung the door open and stepped into the driver's carriage.

She stood inside, hands on her hips.

'Greetings,' she said.

Puck was sitting in the driver's seat, wearing a train conductor's hat. He looked up at Titania guiltily, his hands spread over the controls.

He quickly recovered, and gave her a bright expression. 'Morning!' he said. 'Where can I take you today?'

'Wherever you're going will be fine,' said Titania, sitting beside him and crossing her legs. 'Nice interior,' she added, looking around.

'I changed a few things,' said Puck. 'All aboard? Right. Here we go then.' He blew into a long thin whistle on a chain around his neck, pressed a few buttons and the train juddered into life. Puck squeezed the handle and the cabin plunged into darkness.

For a moment Titania sat silently as the train rattled over the tracks. Lights zipped by at speed, casting a quick-moving glow over Puck's face. He stared ahead with fierce concentration.

Across the carriages a disembodied voice made an announcement over the tannoy: '*There is a good service operating on all other lines.*'

'I hope your holiday has been suiting you?' asked Titania.

Puck kept his eyes focused on the darkness of the tunnel. 'Best I've ever had,' he said.

'That's lovely to hear,' said Titania. She picked an invisible piece of lint from her white trousers. 'We did wonder why you didn't say goodbye.'

'I didn't want to get in the way, with the wedding coming up,' said Puck. He pressed a few buttons and the screech of brakes rattled down the carriages. 'So I just went. No need to worry.'

The train pulled into a new station. The familiar circles of red passed by the carriage windows slower and slower until they were turquoise.

All along the train commuters frowned, mouthing the name of the station.

Titania leaned lazily to look back out of the window. She smiled and tapped her fingernails on the dashboard.

'Mudchute?' she said.

'Yes,' said Puck. 'Well... I liked the word. It's pretty. Imagine sliding down it in the rain.'

He urged the train into action again. He hadn't opened the doors.

As the train raced on again, the logo repeating on the walls gave way to darkness.

'Must be engineering works,' said a woman with a dog.

'You seem a little in your own head,' said Titania.

Puck didn't respond. His fingers flew over the dashboard, pressing buttons.

The tannoy beeped again. '*This train will not stop at the next station.*'

'If there's anything you'd like to talk about…' said Titania. She leaned back to peer out of the window, looking along the platform. As the train rolled bumpily through the station there was just enough time to hear a snatch of jolly accordion music.

'Did you attach this to the Métro?' she asked politely.

'In a manner of speaking,' said Puck. He squeezed the handle and the tune was lost to the screeching of the wheels.

Titania waited a moment before she continued. 'Blossom is worried about you, so is Oberon — and he's hungover so it's even worse.'

'I'm sorry I worried everyone by leaving in a rush,' said Puck. 'Not the plan. If it helps, that's not even close to the worst thing I've done lately.'

'You understand why I've come,' said Titania.

Puck shook his head. 'I can't leave with you,' he replied. 'Not just like that. I'm busy.'

Titania looked over her shoulder at the passengers. People were freaking out. 'Schedules change,' she said.

The train rattled on through darkness. The lights in the carriages began to flicker as the train pushed beyond its highest speed.

'Mostly I'm here to thank you,' said Titania, 'for providing me such good company last night.'

Puck looked at Titania properly for the first time. 'How is he?'

Titania smiled. 'In a wonderful state when I left,' she said.

Puck's eyes were shining. 'He wasn't when I last saw him.'

'I know. You had quite the misadventure.'

Puck operated the brakes again and the train slowed, sparks blaring off the tracks. He pressed a button.

'*There are Scamps and Imps operating this train,*' said the tannoy. '*Please encourage their presence.*'

Puck stared unblinking at the track, his knuckles going white as his hand clung tightly to the handle.

'I was trying to help you and Oberon make amends,' he said.

Puck looked down at his lap, leaving the train to rattle on without his attention. His face glistened with tears, and he took off his driver's hat and flung it into the corner. He rubbed his eyes, ignoring the train controls.

Titania leaned in towards him and spoke softly. 'The others brought him to me in excellent condition,' she said. 'We had plenty of food and stayed up all night and he's currently with Oberon having a lie-in. They're snuggled up together.' She placed a hand on Puck's trembling shoulder, smiling at the thought. 'Wouldn't have turned out that way without you.'

Puck placed his wet hands back onto the controls. His breath became calmer. He swallowed. 'You think?'

'Absolutely,' said Titania. 'And he's so at home. We all think he's great.'

Puck didn't say anything.

Titania raised her head a little, thinking. 'I take it we are between land masses.'

Puck nodded. 'Pacific,' he said. He squeezed harder on the handle.

The tannoy spoke up again. '*Phwoar — you're sexy, secure and pretty! Please speak your longings with us. This is a Central Line train to remember.*'

Puck reached out a hand and pulled blindly on the

emergency brakes. The train screeched into a new station where, once again, the doors didn't open, and the wall tiles formed a wallaby.

A red-faced man screwed up his eyes. 'Is this some sort of fucking joke?' he said.

'I'm going to be late now,' said a different man, sullenly addressing the red-faced man. 'And will they do a refund…' his eyes narrowed.

'Never apologise for your good fairie work,' said Titania. 'We allow what's there already. We're not responsible for the reaction.'

Puck remained still for a moment, then he nodded. His expression had become clearer.

'*Due to dreamlike engineering works, this train is on vacation. Please see station advertisements for details.*'

Titania leaned back in her seat. 'I've got a plan,' she said. 'Bottom still needs to perform at the wedding, and naturally he's nervous. We need to make it safe for him to do so. I hope I have your full attention, because I need a sprite with a cheeky finger.'

Puck held it up. 'I know exactly what you're thinking.'

He started the engine and pulled out of the station.

'We'd better get a move on,' said Puck, cranking the engine.

They drove on and the windscreen began to fog over with condensation. Frost made patterns along the windows, unfurling like a fern on the glass, and through them could be seen a documentary crew in thick insulating coats, filming among a penguin colony. The train delved back below the surface.

'*If you see something delicious,*' said the tannoy, '*secret, sacred, sordid…*' It began to poeticise. '*Pleased moon, right down inside the stars.'*

Puck kept his hand squeezed on the handle and the train juddered through without stopping.

For the rest of the journey the commuters took pictures of the signs as they sped by, and wondered which of their neighbours were actors.

'Nearly there,' said Puck, pressing heavily into the motion of the track.

Titania placed her hand over his. Puck looked down in surprise.

After a moment, he responded to her touch, and they clasped their hands together over the handle that powered the train.

'Does this mean I'm driving?' said Titania.

'To be honest they mostly go by themselves these days,' said Puck.

Titania picked up the driver's hat and placed it gently back onto his head.

'My boy's got a big part, you know,' she said.

'I heard he's also doing a play,' said Puck.

'Good one,' said Titania.

There was a burning screech of metal on metal and the train pulled once more into Bank, forty minutes late. The doors opened and an announcement apologised for the inconvenience, then began singing in Greek.

Everyone tottered out onto the platform. The newly-released crowd mingled into the current smush of people, and everyone stood together to wait for the next train. A man with a cold coffee had written himself an inexplicable reminder on his phone: *Tanya email??*

MILKY WAY

The fabric of spacetime is foaming.

The Hermia nebula travels towards the festivities, flexing lightly as she treads. Her strip-thin superstructure is a string of dust; formed from numberless particles in a mist. Her vapour creates infinite patterns, delicate as lace — and as she moves, they change and alter. Her movements flatter the sky, the great cloud of Hermia spreading over the stars.

Her materials bounce like foam; as faint as single specks of ash. She advances and the ether itself seems to adjust its walls to her. Burning suns dip as she passes. Hermia's speckled edges push out across portions of spacetime, extending it outwards.

She travels at unthinkable speed, her acceleration unimaginable and extreme: a daredevil in the ether, with aeonic dimensions so substantial her rush is made invisible and transformed to a dance of slowness; into just the smallest of breaths as her filaments rise and fall like feathers. A mass such as hers puzzles perspective; how speed is seen. An explorer making a leisurely pace, faster than the edges of the spectrum of light, she exists as an enigma and it's a reputation she's happy to work with.

Buried deep inside Hermia's swirling cloud of stardust, a dozen planets pop into existence like eggs from the velvet darkness. Their lights come on.

Hermia flutters onwards, you'd be forgiven for thinking she must be very light indeed; and so she is. With room enough to envelop whole star systems, part by part she weighs less than Hel3na's rings. She examines her reflection in a curved slice of time passing beneath her, then rolls gently below and examines again from underneath. From both angles she finds the dialogue mesmerising.

But now, a deep and low tremble, transparent in tone, makes its way through the universe and the Hermia nebula realises she is following some quibbling influence, and is obliviously broadcasting herself outwards. Hermia's mass of stardust contains the formation of new points of light, crystallizing gently as they glow hotter. They turn themselves inside out, soaking up the matter deep inside the tumultuous froth of her. Sensitive to every tiny tremor, Hermia keeps course for the gathering up ahead: the busy doings of that celestial collusion of Hel3na, Li Sander and D. Metrius, and her great clouds condense into more solid shapes, much much softer than fluff.

The others, meanwhile, know that somebody new is about to arrive. Each are acutely aware of it. Electrons stand on end and D. Metrius appears augmented, he rotates on a new axis until he identifies the source of this fresh expectation.

—   Party's getting larger.

Li Sander brings himself together until he glows brightly, a piercing single star. He can only watch the oncoming expanse of Hermia's mantle. Seeing how gravity bends around her, Li Sander quivers. They are her target.

Hel3na feels daring.

—   Who's up for this then?

Space boils over with audacious things, but the Hermia nebula brings her own surprises. Here she comes, spooning in the blankness around her, folding in the material, leisurely rolling up all the margins and the infinite strands with gentle power.

The wall of her sets against them. Expectant, the three astronomical bodies abandon their orbits to the flow of her, that plunges everywhere at once. She lingers a little, dragging her cargo over them.

*

As time unbounds itself, they cannot see anything other than Hermia, until they are sunk far into the deepness, lost against the friction of her great dusty pillars. Faster and faster, she blows herself across them. An innocent world of lava soars across the bristling segments of Hermia's inner space, jettisoning layers of itself in a tail of sulphurous smoke. Suddenly every single electron reappears elsewhere, and the whole thing explodes in a cloud of intervals.

Hel3na feels herself heating up — she must be going at a harder speed. She transmits to any nearby stars for an explanation as she keeps D. Metrius in her sights. D. Metrius has gathered enough mass to raise himself up into a new plane of orbit. He forges a precious, unnamed element in his depths, which quickly collapses on itself, leaving its mark.

This makes Hermia compress herself a little.

—   So it's like that is it?

Hel3na's orbit is winding around itself. She performs a steady lap though the regions of the nebula. Meteor showers are drunk down as she spins towards them open-mouthed, all the way past Li Sander.

Li Sander is turning in a restless mobius strip — sending off, every which way. Hermia's surfaces become spotted with precipitation as she senses him, twisting inside herself and pulling her tassels across a new kink in the shape of things.

Hel3na is rolling along the curvature of space. Her orbit is beginning to weave erratically because the path she is on is contorting: her pastel rings are a blur, and steam drifts along in her wake. She feels a striking rise in her core, and sends out a rippling pulse into the cushion of Hermia's gases that is an outcry of alarm and the transmission echoes strangely, distorting into wobbling frequencies, spilling out of its usual range, getting contorted. Hel3na's soundwaves crush themselves into scattered bits. She finds herself pushed along by an ever more forceful pressure of momentum.

D. Metrius, meanwhile, has his own problems. He's growing bigger. He's close to reaching critical mass, madly pulling atoms in towards him. Deep in his core he remembers his earlier temperatures and how hot that seemed. The thought makes him vibrate as he heats up again. His new gravitational weight makes the soft fabric of the galaxy sag. This makes the twisting and bowed path beneath Hel3na buck and kick, and it's all she can do to hold on. She has abandoned all control and submits to the undulations of the blanket of the universe. She cannot escape velocity.

Hermia makes a series of ferocious shapes with her length of stellar dust; whipping from one to another, unable to satisfy herself with any one geometry. She drags her architecture over them in pure vectors, slapping atoms together and sending her occupants into a frenzy.

A new, tight wavelength blasts at full power, fanning out as wide as it can, pushing planets aside to get through, like an urgent warning. It's coming from Li Sander, the binary star. It's barely a wave. It's bent and angular, leaving erratic bursts of noise and bubbles of radiation: the rapid tone of highly alarmed electrons. Even with this disintegration of signal, he's understood clearly. But Hel3na couldn't respond even if she wanted to. As Hel3na moves faster she spins like a dynamo, creating heat, squirting out time — before Li and Sander can even call out, what is about to happen has already happened, utterly fixed and rigid. Li Sander cries out a warning, but it comes too late, and Hel3na spasms into a rigorous death-spin. Li Sander spreads himself apart to avoid a direct collision and, all options exhausted, the uncontrollable gas giant Hel3na bowls straight through him.

The others look on, knotted in the backdrop of Hermia's spiralling gaseous vapours. She lines the horizon and a star deep within Hermia's depths postpones the moment it will go supernova; it will hold back for a bigger burst later. For now its resonances ripple calmly against Hermia's network of stardust, as it clings on.

The two stars of Li Sander hover in place, rocking with Hel3na's indirect impact. D. Metrius's north pole has become his south. His distinctive white shine crackles with sparks of a strong crystalline blue. New thrusts of gravity send him in all directions, tangled in the spidery legs of the Hermia nebula. He tries to paddle back, but their orbits are tightly linked, celestial threads holding fast between them. The future collapses into the past, and everything flattens to now.

D. Metrius radiates the last vestiges of his energy, his dense and round body emitting a pale glow. His heaviness sinks in the middle, bending the spaces around him.

Hermia sprawls out, soaking in the soft tides that come from Hel3na, D. Metrius and Li Sander. The four maintain their connection, sometimes atoms thick. The precise distinctions they once used to tell each other apart are becoming cloudy. They all share something at this moment, communicating with strong transmissions that crease up the firmament and indent the sides of spacetime. Channels of desire make the smallest fragments of space quake and shudder — and the whole universe move to the arising polyrhythms.

Puck's Middle Finger

Quince was sitting tensely on a tree stump with her legs apart, heels grinding into the tightly-packed dirt. Her gaze was directed straight down in front with grim concentration. Lack of sleep made her eyes bleary and bloodshot.

'Right,' she said. 'Either we cancel, or we do the best we can with what we've got. We all want the latter, yes?'

The others were sitting around the clearing exhausted. Their clothes were streaked with mud, and no longer fit properly.

Flute stood up and made a noise of uncertainty. 'I'd love to think we can do it, Quince,' she said, 'but let's face it. What we've got isn't enough, is it?' Her shabby cardigan was stained with blood where she had run past thorns in the night without noticing.

Quince raised her head, and she and Flute stared at each other unblinking. 'There are a few ways of doing this,' said Quince slowly. 'We are not by any means out of options.'

'We have to do the wedding,' put in Snout. 'We'll never do anything this prestigious again.' His hair had become lank with sweat and his cologne had worn off, leaving a salty odour. Snug nodded in agreement, kneeling on the ground, and seeing the movement Snout grew bolder. 'We *must* perform,' he said — his velvet voice had a touch of iron.

'We can make it work,' said Starling, sitting on a fallen tree branch with her ankles crossed. She had removed her shoes at some point during the night, and her feet were smeared with grime. 'We'll only miss the wedding if we have the wrong attitude.'

'I'm not saying I want to miss the wedding!' cried Flute. 'Don't make me the enemy here.'

'I've got a plan,' said Quince. She made a square with her fingers, picturing a miniature theatre surrounded by muddy earth. 'Here's how we do it. Snout is going to be Willy. So Starling, you're Pyramus. Flute stays as Thisbe. Starling, you can't play Pyramus as well as your original part, it's too much, so I'll take that on as well as Lynda.'

There was a pause while everybody thought about it.

Starling opened her mouth to speak.

Snug raised his hand. 'Quince, so you're saying you play Willy's wife, *and* the woman he commits adultery with?'

Snout was already flicking through his script with renewed vigour. 'Could be brilliant. In the scene with the two of you present, the audience's disorientation would mirror Willy's. It has potential to be extremely dramatically effective — if it works.'

Quince nodded. 'A wig should be enough to distinguish the characters. I think there's one in the bag. I'll just have to enter and exit a lot.'

Snout looked down at his script, which was dog-eared and stained. 'I'll need a highlighter in a different colour,' he muttered.

The clearing was beginning to buzz with excitement, fortitude and creative solutions to a problem. Quince stood up from the tree stump.

'You see!' she cried. 'From constraint comes innovation. This could be even better than before!'

'I don't like it,' said Starling. 'Why would you take my character away?'

The lively atmosphere shrunk down immediately into a strained and tight pause. Snout looked up from his script, his eyebrows raised in surprise.

'Pyramus is a main part,' said Quince. 'It's not fair to make you do another part and play Pyramus as well.'

'*You* already have a main part,' said Starling. 'How come you can play two characters?'

'I'd be taking on an easy, small role,' said Quince. 'That's much simpler than having to learn a new huge part in a day. I'm trying to do you a favour! Don't make this difficult.'

Starling and Quince faced each other across the clearing.

Snout cleared his throat. 'We really don't have time for disagreements,' he said.

*

Behind a nearby mound slowly raised the tops of two heads, peering through the tall grasses. A bony finger parted some bracken leaves to point directly at Quince.

'There they are,' whispered Puck. 'Having a group meeting. They didn't even get separated in the night. This'll be easy.' He turned to his companion. 'Are you ready?'

Bottom gulped. 'I think so,' he said. 'Are you sure this will work?'

'It's never failed me yet. And it's a much stronger dose than usual.'

Bottom looked back towards the clearing, where the mechanicals were discussing the new casting. He couldn't make out the words, but even the texture of their voices gave a nervous tightness in his stomach. He wrapped his arms across his body, holding himself closely over the rough denim of his dungarees.

'It's not that I don't trust you,' he said, his voice dry. 'I just can't see myself going out there.'

In the clearing Quince was raising her voice. Bottom's heart beat faster.

He felt pressure on his shoulder. He looked, and Puck was nuzzling the top of his arm, rubbing his forehead into the soft fur. He raised his head and grinned up at Bottom.

'Baby,' said Puck. 'You're ever so warm and soft like this, you know.'

'I do like it,' said Bottom, quietly.

'Well then. Now we only have to deal with the others,' said Puck. 'You wait here: I really won't be any time at all.'

He stood and tripped lightly into the trees. Bottom strained to listen until Puck's steps had gone completely, and his rustling through the bushes had faded into the general sounds of the forest. Then he turned his attention back to the clearing and watched the arguing figures, conscious of his pounding heart.

*

'I'm saying,' said Quince, 'this is already a tough situation. We've *all* had a fright and we're *all* trying to carry on — and we *all* have to make tough decisions for the good of the group.'

Starling stood her ground. 'But why do I have to take on

a part I'm not comfortable playing?' She ignored the loud tuts and sighs coming from the others.

The air was getting strained like an oncoming headache.

'I'll help everybody learn their new lines,' said Flute. 'If we rehearse constantly until we go on I think we can definitely do it.'

'It's not about learning the lines,' said Starling. 'I just don't want to play Pyramus!'

Quince's voice had an edge of contempt. 'What, you think we should let *Snug* play Pyramus? Come on.'

From the tree stump, Snout's laugh was an unpleasant snort. 'You're our best option for Pyramus right now. We're not saying we're happy about it, just that it has to happen.'

Starling spun around to face him. 'You might be happy playing a role like Willy at the last minute but I'm not. I want to play the kind of part I always play.'

'Stretch yourself!' said Quince.

Starling wheeled around again, her expression growing desperate. 'I don't want to do something badly in front of everyone. You can stretch yourself the wrong way, you know. A part like mine I know I can do. I know the lines—'

'For goodness sake, all your lines are *giggling!*' shouted Quince. 'You don't have to do anything remotely challenging whatsoever. Maybe that's why you're so good at it.'

Starling froze, looking hurt.

Snout, Flute and Snug all stared at Quince.

The sun vanished behind a cloud and the brackens rippled as the wind changed.

Quince ran a hand over her hair, which was matted and full of twigs. 'I'm sorry,' she mumbled. 'That was uncalled for.

This isn't about anybody's creative commitment or talents. It's about what's good for the group.'

Starling nodded, biting her lip. 'We're all on edge,' she muttered.

Snug raised his voice over the wind, which was growing stronger. 'Quince is right,' he shouted. 'Let's get behind the plan!'

Suddenly it sounded like the sky was full of tigers.

Quince spoke at her maximum volume. 'I'm the director,' she cried, 'and I'm going to direct us out of this mess! The first thing we need to do is reblock the kitchen scene—'

'What's that?' shouted Snout over the increasing din.

'I said the kitchen—'

'No,' said Starling, pointing up. 'What's that!'

The mechanicals looked up into the tree tops.

The sky above the forest was filled with strange silhouettes.

A dozen bodies were descending, each hanging beneath great propelling blades of huge sycamore seeds, spinning rapidly as they came towards them. The whole clearing was pushed open with revolving force. They drifted slowly past the trees, making the canopy vibrate and shake with the pressure. The hum changed pitch as they came towards the bent grasses and landed on the ground.

They stood in formation, unbuckling themselves from their anchored sycamore seeds. Front and centre was a figure carrying a satchel, wearing an impish grin beneath an oversized pair of goggles.

The bedraggled actors looked at the newcomers, mouths and eyes wide, their argument forgotten.

'Sorry for interrupting another rehearsal,' said Puck. 'I

know they're important.'

In one hand he held an item like a pine cone as big as his fist. He pulled out one of the seeds and threw it into the middle of the group.

It exploded in a shower of pink glitter, sparks and smoke. The mechanicals looked at each other, their faces slack with shock, as their limbs went loose flinging out at odd angles before flopping heavily to the ground, unconscious before they even landed.

Puck pushed the goggles away from his eyes. 'You can come out now!' he called, as he set them on top of his head.

Bottom bounded over the mound and came into the clearing. He looked about at the sleeping bodies.

'What did you do?' he said.

Puck grinned, chewing on a long piece of grass. 'Nothing yet,' he said. He began rummaging around in his satchel.

The fairies went through the group and removed the bottom half of their clothes, rolling them onto their front where it was required. When five bums were raised to the air, two fairies stood beside each one and gave a thumbs up to Puck.

'This is *not* going to help our reputation,' he said, pulling on a thin glove with a snap. He winked at Bottom and went over to the sleeping bodies, pulling a small vial of shimmering liquid from the depths of his satchel.

Puck went between the mechanicals, dipping his finger into the Loveliness and applying it swiftly and smoothly down each bum crack. He proceeded diligently, inserting his finger with care and attention, as if planting crops along a much beloved soil patch.

They moved in their sleep as Puck worked, squirming

141

at first with the feel of warmish slippery liquid inside them before writhing more deeply into the mud.

When Puck pulled out of the final mechanical, the air felt clean and fresh with the sugary smell of Loveliness. Bottom closed his eyes.

When he opened them Puck was striding over triumphantly. He slung his arm round him. 'There you are,' he said. 'All done!'

Bottom smiled nervously. 'What happens now?'

'You wait for them to wake up.'

'And then what?'

'Rehearse the play, perform the play, the end.'

'They won't…?'

Puck shook his head. 'The potion's stronger than that. You might see their faces pull contortions, but that's it.'

Bottom bit his lip. 'It's not permanent though, is it?'

'It'll get you through the wedding,' said Puck. 'After that, we'll see.' The fairies were waiting patiently behind him in a group, giving them both a respectful distance. Puck cast an eye over the sleeping bodies. 'Maybe you decide to hang out with us more,' he said.

'I'd like that,' said Bottom.

'Good news!' said Puck. 'Always happy to help.' And he turned to go.

'Wait!' said Bottom. 'How should I wake them up?'

He looked back over his shoulder. 'Any way you like.'

'Puck,' said Bottom.

'Yes?'

'It's just — I didn't realise it was going to go up their bums.'

'It's the most effective spot.' Puck giggled. 'Where did you *think* I was going to put it? See you at the wedding, Bottom.'

Puck swung his bag over his shoulder and strode off whistling into the trees.

*

Bottom stood alone in the centre of the clearing, surrounded by sleeping mechanicals with their trousers down.

He put his hands on his hips. 'Well well well,' he said. 'This is a fine situation we find ourselves in.'

His fellow cast members did not answer. They were splayed out on the ground, bums to the air. There was a light sound of snoring. Bottom picked his way between them, checking to make sure each one was truly asleep.

'You're all having a nap,' he said. 'Big day today! So this won't do at all.' He scratched his head, pretending to think. 'Maybe I can help.'

The props bag was sitting by a bush. Bottom picked it up and peered inside.

'I expect there's something in here,' he said. He dropped the bag to the floor and squatted down to fish inside, holding it open with one arm and exploring the contents with the other.

'Maybe this?' He pulled out an old accordion and considered it. He wiggled it in front of Snout's face. 'No,' he said, collapsing it gently and discarding it on the floor.

He took a dinner gong from the bag and crept up to Quince with it. 'Hmm... perhaps not.'

He stuck his head all the way into the bag, checking everything inside.

Then he came out again. 'This should do it!'

He stood up pulling out a large bulbous item which was

almost as big as his upper body. He let it dangle in front of him, supporting the weight in both hands.

'This is promising,' he said. He began to untangle it, while gentle snores rolled through the clearing.

The item consisted of a heavy sack made from bladder and several fat tubes of different lengths dotted with regular holes.

'I suppose I just put this here…'

He slung the ancient ceremonial bagpipe over his shoulder and puffed out the bladder until it reached its fullest capacity. When he was satisfied the bladder was at maximum brim he carefully walked into the centre of the group.

He adjusted the bagpipe until he was holding it correctly and breathed in to the full stretch of his beastly lungs. The bladder was vibrating with readiness to expel.

Bottom placed the thickest pipe to his lips and raised his elbow. Mouth full of tube he counted backwards:

'Three, two, one…'

In the Morning (Ding Dong)

A cacophony of ringing bells had the whole city vibrating.

The streets had been hung with flags in imperial colours, and around the necks of golden sculptures of goddesses were garlands of blue delphiniums. The statues of Theseus that peppered the streets had been ceremonially wrapped in pieces of Amazon leather.

Along the beach jogged the Changeling through sea-spray, finishing one final lap of the coast.

Hundreds of guests were already at the Palace by the time they arrived to a great flourish of trumpets. Titania's sky-blue dress trailed behind her as she walked arm-in-arm with Oberon, whose trousers and coat-tails picked up the hue. They wore matching flowers, designed especially.

'We must be on God knows how many social events in as many hours,' said Oberon.

Titania nodded. 'I've stopped counting.'

Bunting fluttered from the ornamental lemon trees. The guests were out on the lawn, some wearing robes of state, others in their very best togas, with wine in hand. The drinks were already poured and stacked in a great pyramid; Oberon took one as they passed. He frowned at it for a moment before muttering something about hair of the dog and taking one more.

'I will pace myself,' he promised, as Titania glanced over his second glass without a word.

The party was crowded with the great and good of Athens, legendary athletes in ceremonial armour, and important visitors from Olympus. A ripple of recognition spread through the guests in dozens of languages as Titania and Oberon stepped onto the grass.

'There's Athena!' she said, nudging Oberon. Swiftly he looked up from his wine.

The goddess was entertaining a group of poets, gesturing elegantly with one hand and holding a spear in the other. She glanced towards them, then returned to her story; with a single word the poets burst into raucous laughter. She and Titania shared the subtlest of nods.

The Changeling was leaning casually against a ten-foot ornamental vase — decorated with a painting of Theseus holding a rock over his head — and flirting with Aphrodite, the goddess of love. She had her helmet under one arm, leaving her hair to tumble down her back, and her robes had a split all the way to her hips. The Changeling gave Titania and Oberon a wave. Aphrodite turned to see who he was looking at, and her face broke into a wide smile.

She gave Titania an enthusiastic thumbs-up, mouthing: *'Gorgeous!'*

'I know, right?' mouthed Titania in response. She and Oberon passed on, leaving Aphrodite to it, and sat down together on the warm marble steps.

'So many old friends!' said Titania. 'It's good when we all get together.'

Oberon nodded as he finished one wine and moved to the

next. 'I'll have to present my compliments to the Changeling at some point,' he said.

'There'll be a queue.'

Titania leaned back on the steps, supporting her weight on her arms, watching the crowds mill about. 'Let's enjoy this moment,' she said.

A trio of Spartan war heroes in dark red loincloths were having an intense discussion about work. They frowned as their conversation was interrupted.

'Excuse me please! Coming through!'

Someone was wriggling among them, squeezing past their huge thighs. Puck popped out from the surprised group of warriors and approached Titania and Oberon with a huge smile on his face.

'Vol au vent?' he said. He held out a pile of pastries in a paper napkin.

Oberon looked at them with interest. 'Kind of you. Are the kitchens open?'

'Hard to know,' said Puck. 'The doors were. Look at this one!' He held it up delicately between his thumb and forefinger, an intricate baklava construction topped with pistachio. Puck popped the entire thing in his mouth.

'Mmm!' he said. Then he turned and sped back off into the crowd.

Titania rested her head on Oberon's shoulder.

'Puck took care of everything,' she said. 'Reassured Bottom, set the whole thing up for today. He nailed it.'

'He's got style,' said Oberon, 'even if he is all fingers and thumbs. Speaking of which you should have him do you a foot rub.'

A young man wearing an imperial tabard stood on the top of the steps and blew into a long gold horn. Oberon frowned and tried to wave him away.

'That's Philostrate,' whispered Titania. 'He's done a lot of the organising.'

'Be that as it may,' said Oberon, and then came the noise of everyone cheering.

Their stately hosts had come out to greet the crowds. Theseus was dressed in elegant white robes and Hippolyta shimmered in a breastplate over a long skirt of burnished gold. They stood at the top of the steps and waited for the applause to finish.

'Well,' said Theseus. 'What a day it is. All of you out in your finest, looking wonderful. Mind the grass please it takes ages to get that stuff going.'

He clasped his hands together. 'No but let me be serious — we are very proud to have you here, and hope the events ahead will be full of delight, entertainment, togetherness and joy. We've had our best people on it.'

Hippolyta continued. 'And the Amazons are looking forward to making this our home as Theseus and I become unified in love and war. Both specialities of mine, as you might know. Fill your boots — free bar for the next four days — if this is your first trip to the palace have a good poke round and there's bowls of sugar lumps if you're planning on visiting the horses.'

Philostrate blew into the horn again, a great fanfare announcing it was time to enter the temple. Titania and Oberon stood to go, their fingers gently touching. Guests were streaming by them up the marble steps.

A drinking song sailed over the bustle of the crowd. It was

emanating from a man coming towards them, with beer foam all in his beard. He reached them and bowed low.

'An utter pleasure, your majesties!' he cried. 'That being said, with you two about is there any other kind?'

'Good to see you, Dionysus,' said Titania. 'And on such a beautiful day.'

Dionysus raised his eyebrows as he scanned the palace grounds. 'So it is, and I daresay you've had something to do with that as well.' He leaned in and put his arms around them both, pulling them in close. He whispered conspiratorially.

'I checked the wine cellars,' he said. 'I must say, they were very good. But—' his voice rose to a gigantic whisper — 'Now they're *better!!*'

Oberon looked delighted.

Dionysus winked. 'See you both at the afterparty,' he said, continuing up the steps.

*

Everybody mingled in the palace grounds. Philostrate was making his way through the guests, sticking his head into conversations with an apologetic grimace.

'What does he want now?' said Oberon.

He bounded up to them to say that Theseus and Hippolyta wanted everyone to gather for a portrait by the temple. There was much confusion as everybody got organised, while Philostrate did his best to direct from the front.

On the highest steps stood the top gods of Mount Olympus, with lesser gods and national heroes below, and the wedding party in the middle; next, visitors from distant city-states;

and Athenians and Amazons spread over the rest of the steps. Sunlight flickered across shields, helmets, spearheads and gilded wreaths dotted throughout the composition. Titania and Oberon were near the centre of the picture, arms around each other, and Puck kneeled in the middle of the front row.

'Ready?' Philostrate held up a hand.

Everyone beamed in his direction.

'Frieze!'

The ornamental fountains burst forth great jets of water, framing the image. Beside Philostrate a group of potters, glaziers and engravers took a rapid series of notes.

'Well done everyone,' he called, when it was done. 'That looks fantastic. Now let's do a silly one.'

*

The many hundreds of wedding guests walked in a merry procession down the great curving path to the city's amphitheatre, a huge sloping semicircle cut into the rock. Soon every row of stone seats had been filled, with the overflow sitting around the top and up the hill beyond. The whole place brimmed with chatter. The lanterns had been lit, creating a mood across the arena.

The wine Oberon had been steadily drinking throughout the ceremony was starting to take its toll.

'When's the banquet?' he said.

'After this,' whispered Titania.

Oberon was looking around for somewhere to buy ice cream when the audience erupted into applause. The Amazons were walking out onto the stage.

They spread themselves out to the edges, each finding her spot. At the front the Amazon who was Maid of Honour stood poised, tossing her spear between her hands. She looked out towards the back of the theatre and nodded.

A bell rang out and the Amazons roared into action.

The audience cheered, some fans whipping out flags. Hippolyta raised her fists in support.

The Amazon in thigh-high sandals danced with daggers against the Amazon with a shaved head, pulling each other in close and dodging blows with split-second timing. They looked out into the crowd at every beat of the action, sticking out their tongues and leering filthily. The audience vigorously shook their flags and banners back at them. The Amazon in silver armour somersaulted across the stage, pulling even more cheering and shouting from the delighted audience by beckoning for it with her fingers.

'Go! Go! Go!' cried the nobles and dignitaries, waving their arms about madly and spilling their wine jugs.

For the finale the Amazons went into grid formation and performed their haka. They moved as one body, their weight fully beared down onto their legs. They slapped their thighs and roared thunderous sounds from the depths of their chests, eyes and mouths wide and open with a chant that channeled fire. High up in one of the top-most rows of great stone seats, the mighty god Ares removed his towering war helmet and placed it in his lap.

The Amazons came together and performed the final positions of the haka while their Queen leaned forwards in her seat — mouthing along with them.

Finally the haka stopped, and they stared into the audience, who for a moment were too awed to make any sound at all.

Then the Amazons raised their arms in appreciation of thunderous applause. The crowd were on their feet, calling out for an encore. The Amazons saluted directly to Hippolyta. She stood, clapping and shouting, tears of fierce pride making her eyes glisten as she punched the air.

Eventually the applause died down as the Amazons picked up their spears, bows and swords, and left the theatre, their arms slung around each other.

*

Chatter broke out across the amphitheatre as the stage was reset. Oberon squinted at the programme.

DEATH OF A SAILSMAN

He turned to Titania, excitedly.

'Theseus was telling me about this! It's a historic arts project on an international platform.' He broke off and stared into middle distance as he tried to remember. 'It's about democracy. He says Athens needs explaining to everyone.'

'Sounds suitably on-brand,' said Titania, a little absently. She was sitting up straight and alert, imagining how Bottom might be doing.

The audience stopped whispering and began to watch a new group of people in black set the stage with focused quiet. With the simple set design of a painted sheet, table and chairs they had suggested a kitchen and many audience members nodded in recognition, noticing similarities with their own villas at home.

While the back row was still gossiping about the Amazon

performance, the goddess Athena reclined further on her stone seat and crossed her legs.

'Time for our great nation to show 'em how it's done,' she said, eating casually from a paper cone of almonds. 'Flipping love the Drama.'

The audience went quiet as a lone person in an apron ran onto the stage. Titania and Oberon both leaned forwards to get a better look.

Quince the painter had a far-away stare. She seemed distracted as she walked around the small wooden table, pottering about with imaginary plates and bowls.

She stopped and faced the audience.

'When will my husband return from his difficult life?'

There was a knock at the door.

Titania's hand found Oberon's and clasped it tightly.

Bottom came onto the stage. He adjusted his shabby jacket and loosened his tie as he walked, and high in the balcony seats there came a light scattering of applause.

Bottom stood outside the door to the kitchen and shuffled his feet.

'So ends another disappointing day in my life,' he intoned. Beneath the exhaustion his voice had a steady confidence. He entered the kitchen.

Titania cocked her head to examine the leading man. Quince stared at him, her face open with sadness and longing.

'I'm so tired, Lynda,' whispered Bottom, his voice easily reaching the highest seats. He looked distant and jaded. 'I have such strange thoughts.'

A wave of stillness began to settle over the amphitheatre crowd.

Snout the fishmonger and Flute the plasterer jogged onto the stage.

'Pyramus! Thisbe! My boys!' cried Bottom. His eyes glittered on the verge of emotionful tears as he pulled them both into a hug.

'Welcome home, Pop,' they said.

'We love having you back,' said Flute.

They all held onto each other tightly.

The goddess Aphrodite made smouldering eye contact with Titania and pointed discreetly at Bottom, mouthing: 'Get a load of *him*.'

Titania nodded back and broke out into a smile.

Aphrodite's eyes went wide. '*Him too?* You legend!'

Titania resolved to make introductions after the show.

A few scenes later, Bottom and Snout were sitting on the front stoop of the Loman family villa. Bottom ruffled Snout's hair with affection.

'And then there's Byzantium,' he said wistfully. 'Byzantium is the cradle of the Revolution. A fine city. And they like me there. I'm telling you, I can drop anchor anywhere and the people know who I am.'

'Sounds great, Pop,' said Snout. 'I'd love to go with you sometime.'

'Someday, Son, I'll take you there. Soon as the tide comes.' Bottom glanced down at Snout and for a beautiful moment they shared a loving look and seemed so contented.

Then Snout stood and left the stage, and Bottom's face sank into the slow recognition that he would never take his son to Byzantium.

The Athenians in the audience were watching closely, their

jars of wine forgotten. It seemed the play was going to address some difficult issues.

Next, Bottom was arguing with Starling the french-polisher. She protested and delayed while he tried multiple times to throw her out of their hotel room. The audience sympathised, not wishing to imagine themselves being rejected by Bottom, and followed with interest as he made his way home to his wife and family.

Quince raised a tentative arm towards Bottom. 'Is everything all right dear?' she asked, her voice tender. She turned to Flute and they shared a look —a dark look that knew all about the whittling knife.

He spoke very quietly. 'Lynda...' He rubbed a hand across his face. 'I dunno.' He stared blankly. 'Maybe I'm not very good at making sails.'

'Don't you say that!' she insisted.

The audience were hooked as the situation in the Loman household grew more tense. Bottom was roaring through his big speeches.

'Instead of giving up on yourself you should hold it down and get up!' He screamed at Snout, who shrank back in the face of his impotent rage. 'And then you might amount to something...' Bottom balled his hands into fists and kicked the table. He spread his arms and stared into Snout, trembling with fury: '*Instead of amounting to nothing!*'

The amphitheatre found itself distressed by the characters' hard lives. Everyone except a hoplite soldier near the front row, who looked about at the bewitched crowds and whispered to his neighbour: 'I'm not getting it!'

He was sitting next to the head of the Corinthian war council.

She frowned a little at the interruption.

'The main character is disappointed in his sons,' she whispered, through tears.

The hoplite blinked with incomprehension. 'So why doesn't he throw them down a well?'

'*Shh!*' The war general returned to watching the action.

After about an hour, Oberon opened one eye. 'Is it over?' he whispered.

Titania shook her head, still focused on the stage. He craned forwards, trying to catch up.

Snug the hosier was walking gracefully onto the stage wearing a black leotard and a pair of false ears. A fluffy mane rested on his shoulders. He stood in the middle and looked out at the audience. They stared back at him.

'When I was seventeen,' said Snug, 'I walked into the jungle. And when I came out, I was rich! Rooooar!' He clawed his hands at the audience, turned and sprang off into the darkness.

By the end of the play most of the amphitheatre were feeling emotionally raw, wiping their tears on their togas. They looked on, gripped by anticipation at how the story would conclude.

The cast stood in a sombre row. Bottom lay dead on his back.

Snout the fishmonger gestured to the gravestone, pointing with his full arm. 'Nobody can blame this man,' he said. 'He's a man who is blameless. He lived the life of a sailsman, always out there in the blue.'

Then the cast went to the front and held hands. A rolling of applause was quickly joined by whistles and whoops. The mechanicals gestured to Bottom and he took a few steps forward to bow on his own, and the applause deepened.

Bottom concentrated on looking at his feet, soaking in that it was all over, hearing the roar of the crowd somewhere beyond the immediate pounding in his ears. When he stood he looked directly at Titania. She met his gaze and they held an intimate moment in that crowded space. Then she bent down to gently shake Oberon awake, and Bottom was overwhelmed by people coming up to shake his hand.

COORDINATES

A watery star goes supernova, several millennia too early, with a sound like a trodden puddle. The water bursts across the galaxy, instantly becoming droplets of crystal and ice that seperate over a heavily magnetised pulsar, streaming close to the event.

The Hermia nebula is distant. Centuries of light away by now. The others watch as she positively saunters across space. As she gathers distance Hermia builds a platform from chocolate-coloured stardust, a granular trail staying behind her like unspooled silk… This is the first line.

Hermia is such a length away that Li Sander, D. Metrius and Hel3na can trace their gaze across the slopes of her clouds as her being comes into view: she floats away, further on, becoming slowly definite and distinct.

They watch across the growing distance as they register the new gaps swelling between them. The atmospheres that separate them are refusing to cool — the heat would melt a comet like a candle.

—   Don't you think this is all happening too quickly?

All four of them are in thrall to the constant motion of the universe, from the florid edges to the middle, playing out possibilities and turning the contents over like a puppy with its favourite rubber chew.

The sky is combusted: a spectacle is being built. Any and every stellar event comes down to how luck strokes, as soft and soluble as tissue paper — as each star is forever wandering their way to whatever's next, perpetually between goodbye and hello, remaining for only now, this groove of collision: the moon turns on a whim.

Li Sander and D. Metrius rest among each other, gold and other precious metals flowing gently between them in an alchemical explosion.

This is the second line: like a seam — adjusting the fabric.

—   Stay a little, he says.

Hel3na manufactures a new powdery gas in her highest hemispheres, and it blows towards the suns of D. Metrius and Li Sander, making a dusty signal of cumulonimbus.

It stays, hung in the ether…

—   Let's pencil something in.

… And this is the third line.

Li Sander unbinds himself, the twin frequencies of his voice are slightly out of phase. Hel3na relaxes her poise. Her glow pulses for a moment. D. Metrius and Hel3na share a segment of wave.

—   That'll do for starters.

A tremor dances on the wind, vibrating through a tight chain of atoms, and each particle shudders in its place.

—   What's this now?

The lines are now joined between them, making a mark. It strikes luminescent across the darkness of space. It beams out — a straight line from Hel3na to Li Sander to D. Metrius to the giantess Hermia nebula: a fluorescent rope pulled taut, its corners locked; a beam of lightness, clear and distinguishable among the softer components in the mute of the fabric.

This new mark can be made out by lucky watching eyes: its angles turned gentle by distance until it registers in some pivotal place as smooth alignment. Anyone looking up at a fitting space and time could distinguish this neat combination as something quite odd: the cluttered sky in sequence.

HEDGE MAZE

Titania put her glass down.

'I'm going to take some fresh air,' she said.

Oberon nodded. 'I'll hold the fort, I think people are about to get in the pool. Plus I could really do with a coffee.'

Titania gave his shoulder a quick squeeze as she stood to go.

The evening light was changing as she reached the celebrated memorial hedge maze. A life-size statue of Theseus guarded the entrance, lovingly carved from gleaming pink-veined marble and holding a drooping animal skin triumphantly aloft. Titania winked at him as she crossed the threshold.

The maze walls towered above, and the sky narrowed until it looked like a long painting of the sky in a dark frame. She trailed a hand along the sides and felt the neat firm leaves beneath her fingers, continuing quickly through its series of navigations. The bustling of the wedding celebrations had been extinguished by the maze's own silence. A light breeze made the walls shudder and Titania's footsteps disturbed the gravel, becoming the only sound.

She turned along a curving path, around a golden vase mounted on a white plinth, then stepped through a subtle break in the hedge — and into an open circle lined with warm stone tiles. Clipped orange and lemon trees stood to attention in deep terracotta pots. In the centre was a huge ornamental fountain that depicted Theseus gripping the horns of the Minotaur and wrestling it into submission, his face contorted with effort, muscles bulging and his legs in a wide, dominant lunge. The fountain had not been turned on, and an inch of still water lay in one corner of the pool.

A figure stood looking into the empty fountain.

'If you're making a wish, do let me know,' said Titania. 'I have a few contacts in the industry.'

Hippolyta turned around. 'Well if it isn't the Queen of the Fairies.'

Her face split into a broad smile, and with a few powerful strides she was at Titania's side, clasping her warmly by the arms.

'Kept seeing you in the crowd,' said Hippolyta. She pulled Titania into a strong embrace. 'Come here you.'

They held each other for a moment, then Hippolyta took her by the shoulders.

'Who'd've guessed I'd end up with a postcode?'

'Athens doesn't know what it's in for,' said Titania with some seriousness. 'Have you received your present, by the way?'

'From you? No, I don't think so.'

'Oberon and I found a Changeling to join your court. A very special one.'

'Oh?' Hippolyta quirked an eyebrow. 'We've not yet been introduced. How exciting! Tell me about them?'

'He's fantastic. I've never known a Changeling quite like him — a completely primed channel to the fairie roads. He's got this whole fitness routine…' her voice trailed off. 'Anyway, he's also a great listener. Plus he's well into Amazons.'

'Oh wow. I can't believe you'd match a Changeling with us!

He'll be warmly welcomed. Can't wait to say hi.'

They stared at the dry fountain. Hippolyta was focused on the plinth tiles.

'The play was intense,' she said. 'Where on earth did you find that actor?'

Titania looked surprised. 'What makes you think that had anything to do with me?'

'He had something of your... charm about him.' Hippolyta grinned. 'And I thought I caught him sneaking a few glances at you.'

Her eyes widened. 'Ohhh I see. No, I did fuck him, but I wasn't involved with the play beyond that. Enjoyed it though. I thought it was well cast.'

Hippolyta laughed aloud and kicked a pebble at the hedge. 'Knew it.'

A gathering of long-dead leaves rustled in one corner of the fountain. Hippolyta walked the perimeter, examining the statue from all angles.

'Who do you think posed for this?' she said. 'It's not Theseus; the back is wrong.'

'Perhaps he gave the artist permission to make a few changes,' said Titania. 'Speaking of Theseus — I've been wondering...' Her voice took on a note of mischief. 'There's a certain.... *thing*, I know would work really well for the two of you. Have you found it yet?'

Hippolyta rolled her eyes. 'There you go. You're at it again. I wish you wouldn't wave it about in front of people all the time.'

'I'm only asking.'

'No you're not: you're showing off.'

'Sounds like you haven't found it yet then,' said Titania.

Hippolyta's eyes flashed with the challenge. 'I'm not so sure you can tell me anything I don't already know in this regard.'

Titania beamed. 'I'm delighted if that's the case! So that must mean—' Titania leaned in to Hippolyta and whispered. Hippolyta became very still.

Titania raised her head triumphantly. 'I just proved I know at least something.'

'That's a lucky guess,' she said quickly.

'Perhaps,' said Titania. 'So I couldn't possibly know about...' she spoke in her ear again, then smiled politely.

Hippolyta paused.

'All right, your highness, you've convinced me,' said Hippolyta. 'Spill the beans then.'

'Shan't.' Titania turned and slowly began to walk towards the exit.

'Hey!' Hippolyta whipped her gold bridal skirt into a scrunch, stuffing it into her leather belt to reveal her bare legs — and the dagger at her thigh. She stood before Titania to block the way.

'Wait a minute there,' she said.

'You'll both have much more fun discovering it!' protested Titania. 'Theseus doesn't know either.'

'You have to tell me now,' she said. 'Consider it an order if you like.'

'Find out for yourselves,' said Titania. 'Consider that my professional advice.'

For a moment the Queen of the Fairies and the Queen of the Amazons stood staring at each other, and above them the darkening sky exploded in colour and sound. They had started letting fireworks off at the palace.

'Let's make it interesting.' said Titania. 'If you've not got it by the year's end, I get your horse.'

Hippolyta's eye twitched. 'You know I love that horse.'

Titania shrugged.

Hippolyta looked over at the statue in the fountain pool. 'You are fucking frustrating sometimes,' she said. 'Come on, let's get out of here.'

They walked back through the maze. A trio of purple explosions spread across the sky, highlighted with shining silver, then the light faded once more to long shadows.

'At least give me some clues,' said Hippolyta.

'Nope,' said Titania. 'You're on your own now.'

'That's not fair!'

'Did I promise fair?'

Hippolyta's hands flopped down by her sides.

'Tell you what,' said Titania. 'Since it's a special day — here's one for free.' She spoke quietly for a minute.

'Is that possible?' asked Hippolyta, eyes popping.

'Sure. What do you think the Changeling's for?'

A whistle soared through the sky and burst into crackles as they reached the statue of Theseus holding the pelt on their way out. Hippolyta gave it a quick pat on the bum as they passed.

Playwrights

Bottom was leaning against a palatial column with his arms folded, holding a cup of wine in his large furry hand. He looked out happily over the crowd, warmly lit by flickering lanterns and the fireworks popping in the sky above them all. He let his gaze dance over everyone, looking idly for a sign of Titania.

There was a polite cough beside him.

'Excuse me,' came a confident voice. Bottom turned to look.

Standing next to him was an elderly gentleman with long white eyebrows that stood almost entirely upright from his face, giving him an expression of perpetual, explosive surprise. Beneath his bony features hung a long white beard, and his chin was raised at a dignified angle that commanded a level of esteem to which he was clearly well accustomed. His toga was pulled tight across his scrawny frame. With assurance he held out a hand for Bottom to shake.

'Highest compliments on the evening's performance,' he said.

Bottom smiled. 'That's very kind of you,' he said. 'I hope we gave the audience what they wanted.'

The man waved his hand dismissively. 'No need for doubt — we were all extremely moved,' he said. 'And as for you! Talent like yours is rare.' He reached into his toga, shuffled around in there for a moment and pulled out a small piece of parchment. He handed it to Bottom. 'My card,' he said.

Bottom took it and read it. His face fell open.

'Aristophanes,' he whispered. He looked up at him and spoke in a voice that was low with surprise and awe. 'But... you wrote *The Birds*. You're my favourite playwright!'

Aristophanes smiled with well-practiced modesty. 'Excuse me while I take a moment to feel self-conscious.' His smile grew genuine and warm. 'I must say I *am* very proud of *The Birds*. You're a fan of the theatre?'

Bottom quickly nodded.

'Look, I'll cut to the core of the issue,' said Aristophanes. 'I'm always on the lookout for fresh talent, and in *you* I sense something particularly special. My new play debuts at the next Dionysia and I'm looking to cast the lead. It'll be a partly devised process, you understand; building the role around the actor.' He looked at Bottom meaningfully.

Bottom mouthed the word a few times before he put his voice to it. 'Me?'

'The very same,' said Aristophanes. 'What do you say?' He placed his hands together behind his back and patiently waited.

A bright note transformed into a piercing whine as a Catherine wheel in the palace grounds spun itself into a wide disc of fire, unleashing a shower of sparks over the onlooking revellers. Then the sound faded away.

'What's the play?' said Bottom. 'Will it be like *The Birds*?'

'It's a new piece, quite different,' said Aristophanes, 'it's called *Rear Window*. It's a tone poem on the nature of voyeurism and we'd like *you* to be the rear in the window!'

Bottom looked at the playwright's card again. 'Sounds intriguing,' he said. 'Will it be comic or tragic?'

'Erotic. In any case there's no need to give an answer now. I'll leave you to enjoy the party — I'll say again, it's a pleasure to meet you. All my details are on there: at least promise me you'll consider it?'

Aristophanes wandered off, rejoining the throng of partygoers.

Bottom smiled and put the card into the back pocket of his dungarees, already knowing he'd be happy to bare his ass for big ideas.

THE BLESSING

There was a queue of chariots backing up along the palace road as countless more guests arrived to celebrate into the evening. A big band of horns, string players and percussionists played enthusiastically from the grand pavilion, and the lawns were full of people dancing hard. From the depths of the largest group of dancers came a steady clap as a circle formed around the Changeling, who was spinning on his head.

There came a cry of '*Pool! Pool! Pool!*' and there was a chorus of cheers. The group of dancers made their way towards the ornamental pond, which was large and rectangular and edged with statues of nymphs precariously holding giant shells. The water was already filled with people splashing about merrily. They waved, beckoning them in. The Changeling stood on the edge for a moment, then stripped in one neat move and performed a swan dive into the deep end. He completed a length and back beneath the surface then rose up out of the water gleaming and wet, collecting his towel from a young man oblivious to having been tasked with holding it.

Drying off his hair, the Changeling approached Titania and Oberon.

'Seven and a bit seconds,' he said. 'Not quite personal best.'

'Well nobody's perfect,' said Oberon, who was clearly impressed.

The Changeling wrapped the towel around himself, a fluffy white loincloth. 'This place has everything,' he said, tying it neatly. 'No question at all — it's going to suit my needs! If you need me I'll be stretching on one of the loungers.'

He gave them a thumbs-up, turned and jogged away.

After a slight pause, Oberon sighed to himself. 'I've missed out,' he said. He looked at Titania. 'What was I thinking? He would have been such fun.'

Titania's eyes twinkled like stars. 'He was. There's still plenty to be had though.'

Within earshot a group of high-ranking dignitaries were discussing the play.

'You know, it actually reminded me a lot of my own Dad.'

'That's funny. I was also reminded of my Dad!'

'Shall we go somewhere a little more private?' said Titania.

'Yes, let's,' said Oberon. 'What's the hour?'

Her eyes flicked up to the stars and back. 'Not quite midnight? Plenty of time.'

She went on tiptoes to kiss his cheek and hand in hand they wandered towards the orchard, meandering slowly between the rows of moonlit tree trunks. Distant music and laughter reached them from the party, but they could also hear each other's breathing. They stood together beneath a low-spreading apple tree with a gnarled trunk. From its twisted branches hung multiple varieties, all shapes and sizes.

Oberon reached above his head and picked one, making the branch taut, then spring back into a gentle flutter. He crunched into the apple.

He offered the fruit to Titania. She bit it as Oberon held it. She chewed slowly, her eyes locked to his. He let it drop to the floor and she could taste the flesh of the apple while they kissed gently. The leaves breathed around them.

'Sweeter than this?' she said.

Oberon placed his hands around Titania's waist, and she let him pull her closer. They laughed quietly, and Titania pressed herself into him as he squeezed, feeling the warmth of his hands on the small of her back.

'Let's bless this wedding,' whispered Titania, and they kissed again.

Titania ran her hands around him until she reached into his trouser pocket. She slowly brought her hand out in a fist, which she opened, palm up, between them. They gazed down at the small vial, its sheen apparent even in the evening's darkness. It carried its own light, casting their faces into half-shadow and lending their skin a certain glow.

Titania opened it and dipped a finger inside, then Oberon took it from her and did the same. Their fingers lightly coated, the empty vial was dropped into the grass beside the half-eaten apple.

Sinking into the kiss, together they moved their hands beneath each other's clothes, feeling over skin and curves until they had each other's bottom in their grip and they found the absolute centre of each other. And finally their fingers gently parted willing buttocks, and each pushed a glistening finger up into the other. His body sucked her in, and she felt her own opening.

*

There is a low rumble in the earth, and a faint drawing made in light slowly begins to trouble the darkness of the sky. And all along the buffet tables, drops of liquid run down between the thighs of the ice sculptures. Over the smouldering boxes of the firework display, the hot ashes curl into knots and rise like bubbles. Fireflies lift and sprinkle colour on the marsh below. Warm air rolls through the orchard, shaking the branches of the apple tree. It catches the hem of Titania's dress. In the herb garden stray dogs begin digging in the dry soil. The beds send up the earthy aroma, somehow stronger than before. And the far-off sound of a hundred horses, clattering in the stables, is a drumroll over the empty amphitheatre, its bare stage watching, waiting.

In the midst of the wedding dancers, a close friend of Dionysus allows the fabric of her clothing to loosen at the seam, and the robe is gradually unpulled and unravelled, streaming outwards, and more skin begins to show in the moonlight and in the flickering shapes from the lanterns. An ember on the wing sails behind a cherry tree and passes an athlete from a distant city-state, delighting in the patter of a handful of guests — eyes glassy, he extends his muscled arms and takes the waists of his acquaintances. In a ring of philosophers, a way of thinking presents itself and ideas linger freely, lost to inspiration. A poet drinks her wine straight from a common jug.

The throb from the orchard moves downwards and out, through the soil and up into the stone walls of the buildings, over the marble steps; it shivers up the columns. It reaches the musicians whose playing intensifies. Now a chorus. Feet begin to jump and spin and stamp into the mud — an impulse that strengthens as groups become crowds under the gathering sky. The stars dance in the mirror of the ornamental pond, filled with guests soaking up the night with drinks in hand. Their wet garments spread out over the bathing pool — a surface of creases that conceal a sea of legs and flesh all mixing in the body of water. Still, between the apple trees, Oberon's lips part, soft from kissing. Long abandoned, the cauldrons are hissing in the kitchens, while tables clack against the tiles. A laundress is tight to a palace guard, both immodest and aflush in the boiling heat of the stove. In a small pantry that shares the wall, the house-keeper and a dapper wedding guest knock together insistently like hummingbirds. A night-time in private, hardly hidden.

Others withdraw. The dark of the hedge maze is holding many secrets, a carnival of sensation. The soft walls house scandalous acts as permissions are atomised. The lure travels outwards. Within the long line of chariots winding their way down from the gates, one carriage seesaws tirelessly, its wheels crunching over the gravel. Flowers open at the wayside as if listening in. The planets dip.

Everywhere the palace grounds are host to its guests with their robes tangled about their feet, stripped of their armour, contorting and bending, mounting, watching, writhing, exchanging, shaped in torch light, surrounded by a choir of groans. Two heavy-thighed Spartan warriors' expressive silhouettes are framed by a cape the colour of oxblood. A party of enthusiastic women run naked across the lawn. The Amazon in thigh-high sandals bends down and slowly begins to unfasten them; she leaves them under a rose bush and makes for a priestess engaged in a willing spree, pious flesh to be clutched under her bare legs. The sky trembles with fireworks and stars. Sparkling figures float down through the air: when they land a dozen new bodies stand among the rest of the celebrants, and with wild shouts the fairies plunge into the sexual revels. Oberon's hand curls in to Titania, pushing deeper into her sex from behind. Her mouth opens in a silent gasp. He slowly removes his finger, playing games of pressure at her edge.

And a guest, struck with inspiration, lifts herself onto the highest wall and cries out words into the night. She recites a fragment, translating as she goes, half improvised and half learned, the delivery of an ancient text held sacred. Four great celestial bodies reveal the constellation, a straight line visible and burningly vivid above the palace: a complement in light and composition that dominates all the other uncountable stars. The bare-breasted figure of the Amazon who was Maid of Honour emerges from a pile of limbs with a headdress dangling from her fist. A lover kneels at her feet, in perfect awe. Lullaby lies recumbent, moving between her legs with a versed palm, upon the steps of the great marble staircase: the whole of the fairie train, in their element, slap bang in the middle of the party guests. The wave comes over them.

Whole swathes of the lawns are obscured by the whirl of dancers. The celebration slowly transforms to intimacy, dressed only in bare skin, hands on shoulders, heartbeats racing. Small piles of clothes in the wine cellars soften the writhing torsos and busts, twisting around, half-cut. Slats in the low ceiling's wood draw slits of lamplight over the subjects packed against the casks, the room awash with must. And to their own cellars, and other private spots, the properties of Athens open, unfasten. The gates ever ajar, neighbours scamper between each others' homes. A night's worth of brief passings in alleyways. Wives running between doors and streets. Ablaze all night this city burns. On the sanded coast, huge bonfires stoked by all four winds are warming the blackness and here, and magnetised, circles of friends cluster, these minutes irrecoverable, hands unreasonable, blood sailing reckless, bodies trembling.

High in the mountains the rivers flow smooth and glass-like from the hot springs, pouring out with fury. The crowded lawns ripple with motion like the surface of the sea. And in the orchard, they barely need to touch. Titania dips her head and runs her tongue lightly down Oberon's neck as slow as they can bear. And every single statue across the world of Hellas is suddenly painted, a glossy new coat adorning the marble, enriching the art.

*

She kissed down over his collarbone and pulled him gently to join her until they both knelt together in the grass. Titania raised her hand and ran it through Oberon's hair, tapping her fingernails lightly on his horns.

'Give me a treat,' she said.

Oberon's eyes widened as an idea landed.

'I love to give you treats my Queen,' he said. 'Especially when…

… I'm invisible!'

Titania laughed and looked around with an expression of surprise. 'My Oberon?' She put her hands on her hips. 'Where *have* you gone?'

Oberon leapt upon her.

Titania arched her back into the dew-covered grass and

Oberon crawled, his lips glancing across her breasts and stomach, his fingers teasing her thighs, stroking upwards and then stopping.

'Wherever are you going next?' she said. She tossed her head from side to side, eyes screwed closed. She laughed and it rang out through the moonlit orchard.

He smiled and lowered himself until his tongue flicked gently through the warm, soft folds of skin between her legs and Titania clasped her hands into Oberon's hair.

'I can feel you,' she said, 'even if I can't see you! Yes! There! My God!'

Oberon held her hips and brought her over, the movement of his lips passing over her tenderly as she surged with pleasure. 'I'm invisible!' he mouthed. *'I'm invisible! I'm invisible!'*

CURTAINS

A new dawn was rising over Athens and the slumbering party guests were scattered over the lawns.

Titania and Oberon were up early, picking their way through the people. Every so often from among the knots of naked bodies came the soft glow of a dozing fairie.

'It's nice to meet new people at weddings,' said Titania. She put a cigarette to her lips and sparked a light for it.

Oberon nodded. 'These lawns are definitely done for, though.'

They stepped over a few Spartans and wandered on, past a couple of upturned Amazon helmets under a cypress tree.

Titania held the cigarette out to him. 'Luscious Woodbine?'

Oberon took it from her and had a long drag inwards. 'Thank you,' he said, as he blew out, and together they watched the cloud rise into the air and disappear.

'You look good with those smokey tired eyelids,' said Titania.

Oberon took another drag. 'Sweet of you. They're not quite doing as I ask,' he said, passing it back. She politely waved a hand for him to finish it off.

'Let's find some breakfast,' she said.

They arrived at a long wooden table with an imposing display of desserts half eaten-away but still standing proudly, like the ruins of an ancient palace. The tablecloth was smeared with chocolate cream and scattered with crumbs, and from underneath a few legs poked out at various angles. Titania and Oberon were helping themselves to cake when a blur passed by with a whooshing sound, and suddenly there was Puck, whistling to himself and pushing a large broom. He stopped sweeping and leant against the handle.

The broom was taller than he was. A jumble of wine corks, theatre programmes and paper streamers piled up against the bristles.

'Your highnesses!' he cried. He gestured towards the sleeping revellers beneath the table. 'Out for the count,' he said approvingly.

'I see you're full of juice as ever,' said Titania.

'Oh yes,' said Puck. 'And I see you two are poaching the last of the cake.' He put two fingers in his mouth and whistled sharply.

'Cake thieves!' he cried. A pained groan issued from under the table.

'It's its own thing, isn't it, having you around,' said Oberon.

Puck lowered the broom carefully to the ground and came over. Then with a neat leap he hugged Oberon's legs and squeezed. Titania smiled at them, taking another bite of cake with a small silver fork.

'Did you enjoy being a wedding guest in the end?' said Puck. 'You said you definitely weren't going to.'

Oberon turned to address Titania. 'Don't listen to him.'

'Anyway look, I'd best get on,' said Puck. 'Once this lot

starts moving about and demanding coffee I'm going to be busy.'

He picked up the broom, used it to bury some discarded party bits under a rhododendron, then walked off carrying it over his shoulder.

The early mist had lifted and light came over the gardens. Flowers were opening.

'How about we go somewhere high?' said Titania.

And then they were sitting together on a sloping hill at the city's highest point, watching the sun come up. They could see all the way to the outskirts of Athens. Meanwhile, the palace was stirring below: more wedding guests were awake, some had started getting dressed while others were basking in the morning air. The moon hung above, a full pale circle, and the new four-point constellation shimmered brightly in the sky.

'Give me your hands,' said Oberon.

Titania cupped them together and he stepped into them, shrinking down to the size of an acorn.

Titania laughed.

She looked down at him. 'I could get used to you being like that,' she said.

Oberon put his tiny hands on his hips. 'It's a gesture,' he said. 'I understand.'

'From which I also benefit, to be honest.'

'I don't doubt it.'

'Your eyes are the same as planets now.'

Titania's gaze moved upwards. 'Look there,' she said.

The four great celestial bodies hung suspended over the palace, strung across the changing dawn sky like a chain of lights.

Oberon lay down. He folded his arms behind his head and stretched out in Titania's palm.

'Beautiful,' he said, looking out. 'Did we do that?'

'I believe we did,' said Titania.

Oberon pondered. 'It's strange to alter things that size.'

Titania could feel her universe alongside a different one. She curled her fingers gently around him and they both fell silent, looking out over the sky.

She said, 'I couldn't imagine it any other way.'

Acknowledgements

A big thank you to die kleine steinfelder galerie.

We'd also like to thank the following
for many kinds of help and support:

Arts Council England, Frances Babbage,
David & Ute, Viki Browne,
Nils Erhard, Emma Frankland, Tim Franklin,
Chris Goode, Amy Liptrott, Liberty Martin, Kelly Miller,
Jane Milling, Juan Carlos Otero, Glory Pearl, Fran Reeves,
Mike Rose, Oliver Sellwood, Jared Shurin, E.J. Swift,
Cat Webb, Chloe Whipple, & our families.

About the Authors

Rose Biggin is a writer and theatre artist. Her short fiction has been published by Jurassic London, Constable Robinson and Abaddon Books, and made the recommended reading list for *Best of British Fantasy* 2019 (NewCon Press). Her joint theatrework *BADASS GRAMMAR: A Pole/Guitar Composition in Exploded View* premiered at The Yard Theatre, toured nationally, and was selected for Experimentica international live art festival. She has been a Miss Pole Dance UK finalist and developed her practice with support from Jerwood Arts. Her PhD in theories of immersive performance was a Collaborative Doctoral Award supported by the theatre company Punchdrunk; her book *Immersive Theatre and Audience Experience* is published by Palgrave Macmillan.

Keir Cooper is an artist working with live performance, writing and music. He was joint writer and a performer of award-winning remix *Don Quijote*, which was selected for the British Council Showcase for Drama & Dance, touring throughout the UK and to Brazil. His other theatreworks include *BADASS GRAMMAR* feat. Penny Arcade; and queer flamenco-theatre on the Spanish Revolution *Republica*, for which he also composed and performed specialised live guitar scores to extended sequences of dance. As well as writing for theatre and film he also writes for jazz-rock bigband A Sweet Niche. He is an associate artist with New British Music Theatre, a collective dedicated to exploring the intersections between these disciplines.

WILD TIME is the second collaboration by Rose and Keir, and their first novel.